Figure Eight

Yard-Sale Karma
Book Eight in the Val Fremden Mystery Series
Margaret Lashley

Copyright 2018 Margaret Lashley

MargaretLashley.com
Cover Design by Melinda de Ross

This book is a work of fiction. While actual places throughout Florida have been used in this book, any resemblance to persons living or dead are purely coincidental. Unless otherwise noted, the author and the publisher make no explicit guarantees as to the accuracy of the information contained in this book and in some cases, the names of places have been altered.

More Praise for the Val Fremden Series

"Hooked like a fish. OMG Margaret Lashley is the best! Val could be Stephanie Plum's double!! Phenomenal writing."
"Margaret Lashley is my favorite cozy book writer. She always gives the reader their money's worth."
"Plan your day around just enjoying every minute. Her characters are so vivid."
"I did not see the end coming. I was totally fooled the whole time."
"Just when I think she can't think of anything funnier for Val to do, she does!"
"I find the characters all extremely unique and entertaining. The author is very humorous and has a great imagination for storyline."
"If you want to kick back and laugh and maybe come away with a simple life lesson I highly recommend you take the journey with Val and her Pals."
"I really love these books. Val and her kooky pals reminds me of me and my friends, lol!"
"Hooked like a fish. OMG Margaret Lashley is the best! Val could be Stephanie Plum's double!! Phenomenal writing."

More Hilarious Val Fremden Mysteries

by Margaret Lashley
Absolute Zero
Glad One
Two Crazy
Three Dumb
What Four
Five Oh
Six Tricks
Seven Daze
Figure Eight
Cloud Nine

"It's easy for the wrong idea to sprout when your mind is full of manure."
Val Fremden

Chapter One

During my half-century on this planet, I'd learned that *everybody* had some kind of secret stuffed away in their closet. Some folks called them skeletons. Others called them boogey men.

As for me, what hid away in *my* closet was made of ceramic.

And it compelled me to do it bodily harm.

"DO ME A FAVOR, VAL. Change your clothes."

My bleary eyes glanced up from the computer screen. I'd been pecking away at the keyboard since 3 a.m., when I'd been throttled awake by a crazy story idea that'd left my mind wobbling around in circles like a gerbil in a lopsided wheel.

Tom, my long-time boyfriend and short-time housemate, leaned against the door of my home office. Blond, clean-shaven, and in a cop uniform crisp enough to crunch, it almost appeared as if he'd been sent by the government to force me to clean up my act.

"Why should I change my clothes?" I argued.

"Because I almost mistook you for a homeless drifter," he said.

Both Tom and the frothy cup of cappuccino in his hand were two temptations I found hard to resist. Still, I always gave it my best shot.

"Nobody can see me, Tom. Besides...these are my...uh...*business pajamas*."

Tom's left eyebrow ticked upward.

"There's no such thing as *business pajamas*, Val. Unless you're a 'lady of the night.' But *you*, my dear, could never be one of *those*...."

"Thank you." I smiled and batted my eyes demurely.

"....because we both know you can't stay awake past 9:30."

Tom drove his jab deeper with an exaggerated wink. My lips twisted into a sneer faster than a barefoot tourist in an asphalt parking lot.

"Hardy har har, Tom. You know, I think I liked you better when you couldn't tell a joke."

Tom pretended to be confused. "Who's joking?"

"Ugh!" I rolled my bloodshot eyes. "You win, okay? Now, hand over the cappuccino before somebody gets hurt."

Tom laughed, gave me the cup, and tousled my nappy bed-head as if I were a child. I took a greedy sip of the delicious brew and watched Tom fiddle with the shirt collar on his perfectly pressed police uniform.

"When you're done with the cappuccino, get a shower and get dressed, would you?" he said. "Go out and see the world. It's still out there, you know."

I scowled. "This never would have happened if I hadn't let you move in."

"What wouldn't?" Tom quipped. "You working at home, or your total abandonment of personal hygiene?"

I glared at Tom. "Like I said before, I liked you better when you couldn't tell a joke."

"And like *I* said, I'm not joking. I'm heading off to work now. Why don't you come up for air, Val...and give the rest of us a breather, too?"

"Another zinger," I deadpanned. "Maybe *you* should be a writer."

Tom shook his head.

"Nope. *One's* plenty enough for this place. I gotta go."

He handed me the morning paper, kissed me goodbye, and disappeared down the hallway. A moment later, I heard the front door close behind him.

I peeked out the blinds to make sure Tom was gone, then I sniffed my right armpit.

Good thing I was sitting down.

Okay. So I've been in my pajamas since Monday. Big deal. That was only two days ago.

I glanced down at the *St. Petersburg Times*. It must have been a typo. According to the paper, it was Thursday, July 18th.

"What?" I muttered.

Four days! Gone by in a blur!

I leaned back in my chair, tapped a finger on my desk, and vaguely recalled a string of hurried, takeout dinners with Tom, followed by typing into the night until I couldn't see straight, then falling into bed long after Tom was fast asleep.

My word count for the week was incredible. But my love life was definitely down for the count.

I sat up and sighed.

At least Angela Langsbury, my writing instructor, would be proud when I showed up to class tonight with my latest story. But if I didn't get a bath and return to the "planet of the washed" soon, Tom and I might soon be all washed-up.

I took another sip of cappuccino and looked down at my computer screen. My gerbil mind took a tentative step on its wobbly wheel.

I'll just finish this scene, and then I'll take a little break....

Chapter Two

The doorbell rang. My flying fingers froze and hovered above the keyboard. I glanced at the clock.

It's half-past noon!

I padded to the door and peeked out the peephole. Either I'd forgotten it was national Wear Every Piece of Jewelry You Own Day, or I was being paid a call by my next-door neighbor, Laverne Cowens.

I opened the door. Laverne let out a little gasp. Her eyes doubled in size, and the crescent of red lipstick below her nose melted like a Christmas candle in a microwave.

"Oh my word, honey! Have you been sick?"

"No," I said, and winced. The sunlight flashing off Laverne's sequined blouse was blinding. I crossed my arms and tucked my fingers under the armpits of my smelly gray t-shirt. "Why would you ask *that?*"

"Well, I haven't seen you for darn near a week...and you look like —"

"I've been *busy*," I said. "*Writing* and stuff, you know."

"Oh." Laverne eyed me up and down. She didn't look that convinced.

I tapped my foot on the threshold. "Did you *need* something, Laverne?"

Her donkey-shaped head raised up until our eyes met again. She flashed her horsey dentures at me.

"No, honey. I just wanted to make sure you saw this."

Laverne poked a pink flyer at me.

"What is it?" I asked.

"Why, it's my favorite time of the year, Val. The annual neighborhood yard sale and bake-off!"

"Oh. Why didn't I get a flyer?"

"I dunno. I got mine Sunday."

I briefly scanned the flyer. My eyebrows shot up an inch. "Is this a typo? It says here that this year's bake-off winner has to *kiss a pig.*"

Laverne snorted. "I know! Isn't it fabulous? I've always wanted to do that!"

I looked at the skinny old woman sideways and, for a second, worried about the state of her mental health. Then I remembered that, given her baking skills, Laverne's prospects of winning the bake-off were as likely as that pig's were of sprouting wings and flying off to New Jersey.

"Are you gonna have a table and sell stuff this year?" Laverne asked.

As I mulled over the idea, my eyes wandered from the flyer and stared absently at the flashy gold sequins spelling out "I Love Vegas" on Laverne's shirt.

If I *did* participate, it would mark my first time doing so. Not because I didn't like a good yard sale, but because until now, I didn't have anything spare to sell.

When my life in Germany had collapsed five years ago, I'd been forced to whittle my belongings down to what fit inside two shabby suitcases. My first hovel of an apartment back in St. Pete had been furnished solely with the junk abandoned by its former occupant.

Then, a few years ago, I'd inherited this house.

Ironically, having been handed a house full of hoarder's junk had turned me into a minimalist. I'd thrown out pretty much everything in the place, and had furnished its empty hull sparsely – namely the same recycled full-size bed and side table that had come with my tiny apartment. To that I'd added a cheap cappuccino maker and a few assorted sheets and towels.

The day I'd moved into this house, I'd left the rest of the junk from the apartment, including a crappy old couch, in the alley by the dumpster. But later that same day, Tom had arrived, dragging that nasty old couch along with him as a sort of gag gift.

Unbeknownst to him, a hitchhiker in the form of a dead finger had come along for the ride. The derelict digit had given me a run for my money with the law, and a lingering fear of used upholstery that some might argue bordered on clinical neurosis.

I'd replaced the finger-infested couch, and, after many attempts to unload my boyfriend, had finally decided to keep him.

Living alone had enabled me to keep things at my house pretty well pared down to the basic necessities. But all that had changed a few weeks ago, when Tom moved in...and brought all *his stuff* along with him.

I handed the flyer back to Laverne.

"Well, are you?" she asked.

"Am I what?"

"Are you gonna have a table at the yard sale this year?"

A grin crawled across my lips like a fly stuck in honey.

"Yeah. I think I will. But Tom's not gonna like it."

Laverne opened her mouth to speak, but the sudden sound of hammering struck us both dumb. We turned and looked down my driveway. The hammering was coming from the residence that bordered the left side of my lawn.

Our new neighbor, Jake Johnson, was pounding a sign into his yard. Perspiration glistened from his bald head. It was late July, so I assumed the rest of him was drenched in sweat as well. But it was impossible to be sure. With the exception of the top of Jake's head, as far as I could tell his entire body was covered in thick, black hair.

The term "swarthy" didn't even *begin* to do Jake justice.

As I watched him beat on the sign post, I couldn't stop myself from wondering if maybe, just maybe, Jake Johnson was the Missing Link scientists had been searching for....

"Hi, Jake!" Laverne called out.

Jake looked over and waved. Short and muscular like an erect chimpanzee, he gave the sign post one more whack, then lumbered toward us, pounding the hammer in his fist as if he were practicing for his next target.

If Laverne had known everything *I* knew about our primitive neighbor, she'd have pirouetted on her gold high heels and fled for the hills.

A couple of months ago, Jake had been released from prison after serving twenty years for arson. And...uh...for barbequing his mother. According to newspaper reports, Jake had used a bedroom in his house next door as a kind of makeshift crematorium.

Most folks around here thought Jake was guilty as sin. But a few believed that his mother had been a victim of spontaneous combustion, and that he'd been wrongly convicted.

I was among those few.

Still, I had to admit, Jake had a rather worrisome penchant for outdoor grilling....

But whether Jake had been guilty or not, I would forever be indebted to him. During his time in the slammer, he'd earned a degree in pet psychology. Since his release, he'd put his new-found skills to work, helping skittish, incorrigible canine clients overcome their neuroses.

To non-believers, dog psychology may have sounded as preposterous as spontaneous combustion. But not to me. Not *anymore*, anyway. Not long ago, Jake's unorthodox "primal howl" treatment had cured me of my fear of wedding rings, thus enabling me to lead a more full and productive life.

A smile curled my lips. The memory of sitting around a fire, howling with a poodle in Jake's backyard warmed my heart. I waved at my therapist as he crossed the yard.

"Howdy, neighbor," I said.

Jake had barely gotten within arm's length of us when Laverne jabbed the pink flyer at him.

"You having a table this year?" she asked, wriggling as if her bladder were about to burst.

"I dunno. Don't got much to sell," Jake replied in an accent that reminded me the urban-dwelling ape-man once hailed from Jersey.

Hoboken-habilis.

Jake glanced to his left, then right, then pounded his fist palm with the hammer. As he looked me and Laverne up and down, I almost expected him to break out into a chimp mating call. But he lowered his gravelly voice and spoke in a half-whisper instead.

"You's guys, I think we got a thief in the 'hood. You know, that's the third sign I've put up this week. I get up in the morning, and, like, 'poof,' the sign's gone."

"What's it for?" Laverne asked. "The yard sale?"

"No. My animal therapy business."

"Huh. That's weird," I said.

"Animal therapy's not weird," Jake said defensively.

"No. I mean it's weird the signs are going missing," I said.

"So, you're not having a table, Jake?" Laverne whined, her face as fallen as a drop-kicked soufflé.

Jake shot me a quizzical look. I shrugged and mouthed the words, "Laverne loves yard sales."

Jake cleared his throat. "Well, hey, I can probably scrounge up a table. I mean, who ain't got junk? Or I'll *buy* something, for sure. You never know what you'll find at a yard sale."

Laverne's dentures beamed like pearly headlights. "That's right, Jake! That's the best part! Finding all the hidden treasures! Oh! I'm so excited I can hardly wait!"

"Yeah," Jake said, and looked at the flyer. "But I ain't too keen on this bake-sale thing."

My gut gurgled. I eyed Jake and shook my head ever so slightly. But it was too late.

"Why not?" Laverne asked. Her worried, pug eyes shifted back and forth between me and Jake.

"Personally, I think making a pig kiss a person qualifies as animal cruelty," Jake said.

Laverne put her hands on her hips and cocked her horsey head sideways.

"Well, now," she said, "I guess that would depend on what kind of person the pig had to kiss."

Chapter Three

When Laverne rang my doorbell at half past noon, I'd been deep in the "writing zone." I'd almost finished my latest story, and I was desperate to get back to my computer before I lost my mojo.

As the old saying goes, "Desperate times call for desperate measures." So, I got rid of the noisome pair by employing the newly acquired super-power of my crime-fighting alter-ego, Valiant Stranger.

Like Godzilla run amok in the suburbs of Tokyo, Valiant Stranger raised both arms and blasted out a mushroom cloud of body odor that nearly brought Jake and Laverne to their knees.

It was rude, I admit.

But highly effective.

No sooner had I raised my elbows level with my ears than Laverne's face shriveled like a powdered prune. She mumbled something about having to get back and rearrange her silverware drawer, and took off toward her house.

Jake bowed out too, without bothering to offer an excuse. I imagined him needing to return to his Neanderthal lair to keep the home fire burning – just as I needed to get back to my writing cave before my inspiration fizzled out. I wondered if his lair smelled as bad as *I* did....

BY HALF-PAST THREE, I'd finished the final draft of a short story I'd started a few weeks ago called *Golden Years*.

I typed, "The End," saved the file, and closed my laptop.

A satisfied grin spread across my lips. "The" and "end" had become my favorite new words.

I reached across my desk and pulled the lid off a jar of jellybeans. I plucked out a popcorn-flavored one and popped it into my mouth as a reward for a job well done...or, at any rate, *done.*

As I put the lid back on the jar of treats, a card pinned to the corkboard on the wall above my desk fell off and landed on my computer.

It was the dreamcatcher postcard my friend Goober had sent me a week or so ago, right after he'd disappeared.

My teeth gently chewed the buttery jellybean as I studied the glossy photo. It featured a beautiful, feathery dreamcatcher hanging from a country porch above a set of comfy-looking, pillow-laden rocking chairs. I re-read the accompanying inscription for the millionth time:

I hope all your dreams come true.

The sappy sentiment made my nose crinkle.

Horse crap!

Goober wasn't the sentimental type. Neither was I. I imagined him laughing at the thought of me reading the postcard. He knew darn well I'd gag on its sugary sweetness.

Still, the mere thought of Goober caused a small ping of pain in my heart.

I blew out a breath and flipped the postcard over. It wasn't the postcard image that haunted me. It was the unsigned note Goober had scrawled on the back.

If you ever need me, you know how to catch me.

The problem was, I didn't.

How could I "catch" Goober? The last time I saw his dumb, peanut-shaped head was at the Polk County Police Station in Lake Wales, a good eighty miles or more from here. I'd stood in the parking lot and watched him take off down State Road 60 in Cold Cuts' old Minnie Winnie RV.

At the time, I'd thought he was heading back to St. Pete like I was. But he'd never showed. Instead, he'd just up and disappeared, without telling me where he was going, what he was up to, or how in the world he'd earned that mysterious check for ten grand.

I studied the postmark on the card for a clue. Goober had mailed it from Greenville, where my adoptive mother, Lucille Jolly Short, lived. Did he do that so no one would suspect the postcard was from him? If so, why was he concerned about that?

The only thing I knew for certain about Goober was that right before he disappeared, he'd saved me and himself from an angry mob of RV'ers. So, I could safely assume he didn't have a death wish...

...and neither did *I*.

As I pushed the pin into the soft cork, the odor emanating from my armpit nearly knocked me over. Before I asphyxiated myself, I switched off my computer, peeled off my stinky t-shirt, and headed for the shower.

I WAS PULLING A FRESH shirt on over my head when a glint from the bedroom window caught my eye. It was the late afternoon sun ricocheting off a beer can twirling from a piece of fishing line.

The can was part of the ridiculous "redneck dreamcatcher" Goober had surreptitiously gifted me right before he took off for parts unknown. Tom had found it in Maggie's backseat when I returned from Lake Wales, and had hung the abomination on the curtain rod above our bed as a joke.

But it didn't seem that funny anymore.

I stared at the crude creation. It looked like something an unlucky angler might catch if he went fishing in a trash bin late at night...outside a strip club.

Goober's "redneck dreamcatcher" was nothing more than a wire clothes hanger that'd been bent into a misshapen circle. A pair of women's neon-pink, thong underwear had been stretched across the wire circle like a pimp-inspired Mercedes logo. A trio of empty tin cans swung from the bottom of the hanger on fishing line. Namely, two Pabst Blue Ribbon beer cans and a Skoal chewing tobacco tin.

I shook my head at the monstrosity.

Whoever'd come up with that lousy idea obviously didn't have a clue *about...*

Wait a minute! Clue. *Maybe* the dreamcatcher *held the clue on how to "catch" Goober!*

Like a naughty child, I climbed up on the bed and jumped up and down on it until I could reach the wire hanger and knock it free from the curtain rod. On the third try, I dislodged it and the dreamcatcher tumbled on the bed at my feet. I knelt beside it and shook each beer can and the tobacco tin. Nothing rattled around inside any of the empty cans. That left only one last place to look.

Crap. I was going to have to touch those nasty panties.

I winced, and cautiously flipped the tag up on the thong underwear. Clinging to the backside of the label was a little circular sticker that read, "INSP 13."

I let go of the tag. My heart sunk. Not just for me, but for poor "Inspector 13." Whoever he or she was, I wouldn't want to trade places with them for anything in the world.

Checking the so-called "quality" of cheap thong panties for a living?

Poor sap.

If it weren't for bad luck, they'd have no luck at all.

Chapter Four

"You ready to go?" Laverne asked over the phone.

"Sure. Meet you out front."

I inched my feet into some sandals and headed for the front door. It felt good to be getting out of the house.

Ever since I'd left my job at Griffith & Maas and launched my work-at-home writing career, my social life had shrunk to near molecular level. I figured there were probably amoebas out there somewhere having more fun than me.

Without the regular work lunches I used to have with my boss and friend Milly, my weekly calendar had been reduced to the occasional chat with Laverne over the fence, grocery shopping, and a Thursday-night class called *Mystery Writing for Fun and Profit*.

As a fledgling novelist, aka masochist and self-inflicted shut-in, the weekly writing workshop had become my new professional touchstone. That didn't sound too bad until one found out the workshop was just a two-bit continuing education course attended by a three middle-aged wannabees.

Four, if you counted the instructor.

So far, the *fun* part of the class hadn't shown up yet. I hoped the *profit* part would...and soon.

In fact, I was banking on it.

Writing had become my sole source of income. And to date, it had earned me exactly diddly squat.

It had been Laverne who'd turned me on to the writer's workshop at St. Pete College last month. She'd been taking a baking class there. As fate would have it, her class met the same day and time as the writing workshop. So, she'd been hitching a ride with me.

Over the past few weeks, the whole thing had blossomed into a mutually beneficial arrangement. Laverne got a free ride to class. In return, when we got back home, I got to practice my free-throw by tossing her noxious baked goods into the trash bin in my garage.

I liked to think I was getting a little exercise, and saving lives at the same time.

"THANKS FOR THE LIFT," Laverne said as she unfolded her long legs from the floorboard of Maggie's passenger seat and clonked her high heels onto the asphalt parking lot. "See you after class."

I watched the skinny old woman toddle away on sparkly, six-inch heels toward her classroom, then I grabbed my folder and notebook and headed to my writing group.

As I walked into class, I couldn't help but notice the olive-drab color on the walls blended naturally with the sour expressions of the two other students, Victoria and Clarice. The duo of dowdy dames stared at me blankly, without so much as a nod "hello."

Our instructor, Angela Langsbury, a scrawny old woman with skin as blue-white and translucent as skim milk, grabbed a No. 2 pencil from a cup on her desk.

"Well, Ms. Fremden, how does it feel?" Langsbury asked. She sat on the front of her desk and listed slightly to the left, as if at any given moment she might collapse onto the floor.

"Excuse me?" I asked.

Langsbury began to absently poke the pencil into her matted gray hair.

"How does it feel to have your first published story?" she asked.

Employing the pencil like a small, yellow spear, Lansbury jabbed it around inside her helmet-shaped coiffure, which had been rendered stiff as coconut fiber from repeated, liberal applications of Aquanet. She employed the hurricane-strength hairspray before, during, and after each class. Every time I entered the room, the pungent cloud of hair lacquer stung my eyes, burned my throat, and coated my lungs.

"Published?" I coughed. "What do you mean?"

I watched in morbid fascination as Langsbury's stabbing pencil dislodged a cascade of dandruff. It rained down over her shoulders like her own personal snowstorm, and freckled the sleeves of her battleship-gray jacket.

"Yes, *published*," she said.

I took a seat. Langsbury put down the pencil, grabbed a newspaper from her desk, leaned forward, and jabbed a boney finger at an article she'd circled with a red marker.

"This *is* you, isn't it?"

I tore my eyes away from the blizzard of dead scalp cells, bit my lower lip, and allowed myself a proud grin. Printed in the newspaper, right next to a picture of a watermelon carved into the shape of a piglet, was *The Fiction Fables* column...with my name at the top!

"You saw my article," I said.

"Of *course*," Langsbury replied. "Why keep it a secret? Or should I say, a *mystery?*"

I had my reasons. The main one being the backstory was too... well...*complicated and embarrassing* to explain.

A little over two weeks ago, I'd run off to Polk County for a "writer's retreat" at a trailer park called Shell Hammock. The trip had provided inspiration galore...but it had also gone, shall we say, a tad *awry*.

Long story short, after arresting me and confiscating my computer for incriminating evidence, the Polk County Chief of Police had been impressed with the story he'd found on my hard drive – *The Snickerdoo-*

dle Murders – especially when he'd discovered it was a work of fiction, and not the sick machinations of a psychopath's maudlin memoire.

Chief Collins had shown my story to the editor of *The Polk County Poker*. With my permission, *The Snickerdoodle Murders* had run in yesterday's lifestyle section. Being as the paper was published in another county, I didn't think anyone in St. Pete would ever see it.

I'd been mistaken.

"So, how does it feel, Ms. Marple?" Langsbury quipped.

"Feel?"

"Hello? Yes, *feel*. How does it feel to be published for the first time?"

"Oh." I sat back in my chair. "Well...to be honest, I feel kind of *exhilarated*."

I sighed as I struggled to define my mixed emotions.

"But I also feel kind of *exposed*. You know? Like I've just run down a crowded street naked...with my hair on fire."

Langsbury laughed. "Then it feels as it should."

The old woman rested her rear-end on the top of her desk, looked up at the ceiling dreamily, and sighed.

"Being published is like making love, class," she said. "The first time is always the most memorable, but certainly not the best you'll ever have."

Someone coughed, shattering Langsbury's philosophical moment.

Langsbury angled her helmet head at us, her scrawled-on eyebrows crooked into a sharp triangles. Her intense, beady eyes locked onto their target and her mouth fired.

"Unless, of course, you were dumb enough to go and marry your high-school sweetheart."

Victoria, a frumpy gal with dark glasses and the face of a frustrated librarian, choked on the sip of water she'd just slugged from a bottle.

I glanced over at Langsbury. She was studying Victoria like a lab specimen, one side of her mouth curled slightly upward. Suddenly, the old woman's head jerked left. She faced me head on with an oddly menacing look that made me squirm in my seat.

"Too bad my star pupil won't be going to the writer's retreat with us next weekend."

Clarice, the only other student in the class, sniffed through her thin, pinched nose. I looked over just in time to catch the remains of the dirty look she'd shot my way.

"I have...uh...other commitments," I said.

It was a lie, of course. I wasn't about to pay eighteen-hundred bucks to play *Murder She Wrote* with a geriatric plagued with debilitating dandruff, a bookish goody-two-shoes, and a snobby, humorless twit.

"So, what do you have for me this week, Ms. super star?" Langsbury asked.

"Uh...a story about a woman who retires to Florida," I said. "To live out, you know, the best years of her life."

I handed Langsbury my manuscript. She looked down at it and sighed.

"*Golden Years?*" she grumbled. "What a butt-load of fiction *that* is."

CLASS LET OUT EARLY, and I got bored waiting for Laverne to show up. To pass the time, I put the top down on Maggie and looked up at the stars from the beautiful ambiance often afforded by inner-city parking lots.

The late-July night was as warm and humid as a sauna. But the sky was unusually clear. I tried to focus on the twinkling lights blinking on and off in the stratosphere, but I kept getting distracted.

Nearer by was a sideshow that was hard to ignore.

In front of me, buzzing around within the yellow haze emanating from the street lamp overhead, was a thick, swirling mass of nocturnal insects.

It's true. Everyone on the planet is partying more than me....

I leaned back in Maggie's driver's seat and tried to imagine myself as part of the "in" insect crowd circling the light.

Were the bugs having a rave? If so, was that mole cricket the host? Were they all drunk on nectar? Why else would they swarm around in a giant vortex of fellow flying invertebrates? And why this lamppost? Was it the latest cool nightclub? Were they dancing? Was that huge, fuzzy moth buzzing around the perimeter a bouncer?

"What'cha doin' honey?" Laverne asked from the darkness.

I nearly jumped out of my skin.

"Uh...watching the local fauna," I replied.

"Honey, that's not very ladylike."

My brow furrowed for a second, then I let it go along with the need to understand Laverne's thought processes...or lack thereof.

"Sorry," I said as Laverne climbed into the car like a huge grasshopper covered in glitter. A weird feeling shot through me, as if my earlier thoughts of disco-dancing bugs had conjured Laverne into reality.

"How was class?" I asked

She laughed. "No fist-fight tonight, so we're making progress."

Laverne reached for her seatbelt, then froze. She stuck a hand underneath her rear-end and pulled out the newspaper I'd absent-mindedly left on the seat.

"What's this?" she asked, and held up the article in *The Polk County Poker*.

"Oh." I felt my cheeks flush. "It's just a little story I wrote."

I snatched the article away. I didn't want Laverne to know her mortiferous cookies had been the inspiration for my tale of murder and mayhem.

Laverne reached a long, thin, insectoid arm over and snatched the paper back.

"This is *you*, honey!" she said, as if I hadn't realized it. "Why, you should be proud!"

She studied the paper a moment and read aloud, "*The Snickerdoodle Murders.*"

She looked at me funny. Like a confused beetle.

"I thought you said you were gonna call your story *The Snicker* Bar *Murders.*"

"I thought about it," I backpedaled. "But then, you know, *everybody* loves snickerdoodles!"

Laverne beamed at me. Her dentures shone white in the dark like an albino corncob under a black light. Or maybe a grinning praying mantis.

"You know, you're right, sugar," she said. "Everybody *does* love my snickerdoodles. You know what? You've got me to thinking. I'm gonna make a double batch for the yard sale on Saturday!"

"Oh, goodie," I said and turned the key in the ignition. "I bet they turn out to be the talk of the neighborhood."

Chapter Five

I stared at the plastic potato peeler in my hand.

"To peel or not to peel?" I mused aloud.

The green-handled device was one of a pair we owned, now that Tom's stuff had *invaded*...

Be nice, Val!

...correction, *had been added to* – the household.

A wave of claustrophobia washed over me. Tom's clutter was closing in on me like a two-headed monster.

I sucked in a deep breath and tried to look on the bright side. At least when it came to big-ticket items, Tom and I didn't have any duplicates. As part of the move-in agreement, Tom's bed had been relegated to the dumpster – along with whatever "memories" it held in its foam. Since I'd just gotten a new couch, his old sofa had gone to live with one of his newly divorced cop buddies.

Still, I was riddled with an unnamable apprehension. So many little things had snuck past my watchful eye...like the potato peeler I now held in my hand.

Like stowaways hidden in the recesses of Tom's moving boxes, they'd begun to appear in drawers and on shelves and countertops – like mice, silverfish and other uninvited household pests.

The kitchen had proven to be the worst. With the addition of Tom's stuff, we now had double of nearly every cooking gizmo and gadget ever invented by Ronco, Shark Tank and the Home Shopping Network.

Tomorrow's yard sale would be the perfect time to get rid of the redundancies. I mean, who needed *two* potato peelers – or egg scramblers, for that matter?

But then again, if things didn't work out....

I bit my lip and put Tom's potato peeler back in the drawer, just in case.

Stop it Val!

You can't keep on living with one foot on a bright future with Tom – and the other on the rotten banana peel of a relationship fated for the skids....

I sighed, clenched my jaw and set both feet firmly into the future with Tom. I fished the potato peeler back out of the drawer and put it in the jumbled pile of other gadgets I'd heaped onto the kitchen counter.

It was the right thing to do. Still, the effort made me wince.

I HEARD THE FRONT DOORKNOB jiggle, then the door open.

"Val! I'm home!"

"I'm in here, Tom."

Tom poked his handsome face into the kitchen, shot me a boyish grin, then swooped in and cornered me by the fridge for a kiss.

"Happy start to the weekend," I said.

"It will be...when you move out of the way and let me get a beer."

Tom reached around me and opened the fridge. I wasn't sure if he was joking or the honeymoon was finally over.

"Har har," I said. "Another joke, I hope."

Tom kissed me. "You'll always be cuter than the St. Pauly's girl."

I eyed him suspiciously. "So, what's up with you, Tom? Have you been taking 'funny cop' classes?"

Tom grinned. "Hey. You've got your secrets. I've got mine." He grabbed a beer from the fridge. "You want one?"

"Sure."

Tom handed me the beer already in his hand and took out another, then perused the pile of gadgets littering the kitchen counter.

"Yumm!" he hummed. "Looks like you're getting ready to cook up a storm."

I took a draw on my beer. "Uh...not exactly."

Tom's grin collapsed.

"Aww, crap," he said. His expression when serious and he locked his eyes on mine. "Is there something you want to tell me, Val? Come on. You don't want me to *move out*, do you?"

"What? No! I'm just gathering things up...you know...for the *yard sale* tomorrow."

Tom's face went slack with relief.

"Good," he said, and blew out a breath. He smiled at me for a second, then his eyebrows crashed together in the middle of his forehead. He looked down at the pile of gadgets on the countertop.

"Wait a minute," he said. "This is all *my* stuff!"

I feigned innocence. "Is it? I hadn't noticed."

"Come on, Val. That's hardly fair."

"Well, we don't need double of everything anymore. And your stuff is...uh...*older*."

Tom eyed me for a moment, then a smile broke out on his face big enough to dimple his cheeks.

"Are you *sure* you don't want to keep a spare, Val? You know...*just in case things don't work out?*"

Dang. Sometimes it was downright scary how well that man knew me.

"I'm sure," I said, not absolutely, totally, one-hundred percent convinced. But then again, would I ever be?

Tom grabbed me up in a bear hug and kissed me on the nose.

"Well, in that case," he said, "*you* decide what stays and goes. I don't care what you get rid of, Val, as long as you keep *me*...and I get to keep *you*."

"Great," I said, wriggling in Tom's boa-constrictor squeeze. "Then could you do me a favor?"

"Anything."

"Help me move that old chair of yours to the curb."

Tom let loose of his hug. I nearly tumbled to the floor. His face switched to unreadable cop mode.

"Which chair?" he asked.

I pointed to the hideous Barcalounger sitting in the middle of my living room. It had been festering there like the world's ugliest toadstool since Tom had dragged it into the house along with the rest of his stuff.

My nose crinkled at the mere sight of it. The horrid thing was upholstered in that detestable, brown-plaid fabric that seemed, like flypaper, to lure men by the millions to the demise of their homes' décor...*and* their love lives. One look at that fabric was enough to extinguish a woman's libido from twenty paces.

I stared at the tattered, mustard-brown flaps covering the armrests. They were, sadly, the chair's most redeeming feature.

"*That* one," I said, and pointed to the ugliest five-hundred-pound gorilla that ever dared enter a room.

Tom crossed his arms.

"Look, Val. You can get rid of *everything else I own* – but *not* my chair."

My lips puckered until they nearly met my nose.

"Why?" I whined. "What's so great about that old hunk of junk? We can get you a *brand new* one...one with a cup holder...and *massage* action. You know, like Winky's got."

Tom shook his head like a spoiled child. "No."

"But *why?*"

"I have my reasons."

"*What* reason? Did your mom give birth to you in it?"

Tom shot me some side-eye. "No. But you're on the right track. I want to keep it for *sentimental* reasons."

"Tom, don't you realize that upholstery's been banned in eighty nations?"

Tom's usually calm, sea-green eyes began to gather clouds. His shouldered stiffened.

"Listen, Val. I don't ask you to give up *your* weird stuff."

Say what?

I crossed my arms, mirroring his defiant stance. "*What* weird stuff?"

"Well...those figurines on the mantle, for one. And all the other ones you collect, just so you can smash them with your so-called, 'Hammer of Justice.'"

My ears burned. "For your information, the figurines on the mantle are *family*. The others are...*therapeutic*."

"Therapeutic?" Tom snorted.

"Yes. They provide...*stress relief*."

Tom stifled a smirk. "I *see*. Well, how about a little trade, then?"

"A trade?"

"You give up your figurines and I'll give up the chair."

"Tom!"

"That's my offer. Take it or leave it."

My mind whirled like a tornado in the trailer park of love.

What had I been thinking? Why had I let Tom move in? Relationships involved compromise. I was absolutely rotten at it.... Give up my figurines? No way! Good thing I hadn't sold all his stuff yet. And some of Tom's moving boxes were still in the garage. But then again, next time there was a spider in the bathtub....

Oh, crap on a cracker!

"Deal," I said. "So, help me move the chair out of here."

Tom held a palm up like a traffic cop.

"Not so fast, missy. First you have to *prove* you've given them up."

"*Prove* it?"

"Yes."

"What do you mean?"

"I mean you can't smash a single figurine for, let's say...*a month*."

"*A whole month?*"

If I'd have been chewing gum, I'd have swallowed it.

"That's how long it takes to form a new habit," Tom said, then shot me a smug smile. "Last that long without hammering a Hummel and I promise I'll have my chair hauled away."

I stared at the hideous chair, then thought about my stash of figurines secreted away in the bedroom closet. It wasn't fair! At least I had the decency to keep my dirty little secrets out of view!

I pouted like a pre-teen who'd just lost her Malibu Barbie to the rich girl who already had two Dream Houses and a Ken doll in a tuxedo.

"Okay," I grumbled.

Tom smiled in a way that made me feel as if I'd already lost the bet. *What a jerk!*

"It's settled then," he said, and raised his beer bottle.

I raised my bottle toward his. But I didn't hear the clink as they met. My mind was too occupied with other thoughts.

Oh, it's settled all right, Mr. Foreman. Bring it on! Pucker up, because you can kiss that rotten old lump of a chair goodbye!

Chapter Six

I barely had time to finish my cappuccino this morning. Breakfast was a gobbled-down slice of toast with a slap-dash smear of peanut butter, finished off with a hasty peck on the lips from Tom.

"You ready for battle?" he asked as I scurried past him in the kitchen on my way to the garage.

"As ready as I'll ever be. Wish me luck!"

He shot me a thumbs up as I opened the garage door. I nearly swooned. Even at the eye-wateringly early hour of 7:15 a.m., the garage was already heating up like the backseat at a drive-in movie. I hit the button for the door opener. As the double doors grunted and groaned their way toward the ceiling, a hot, humid breeze wafted in and instantly melted last night's mascara.

No doubt about it, it was going to be a scorcher.

But there was no time to worry about glamour. I was under the gun. I grabbed the folding table against the wall and dragged it down the driveway to the sidewalk. Sweat trickled down my back as I fumbled with its metal legs. Three unfolded easily. The last one stuck halfway down and refused to budge another inch.

Great. Just what I need!

I tugged at the stubborn leg until I grunted from the effort. My hands began to tremble.

Hurry up, Val! There's no time to waste!

"Stupid table!"

I reared back and kicked the ornery leg. It squealed and popped into place like an out-of-socket hip bone.

"Aha!" I cheered, and flipped the table upright. I checked my cellphone. It was 7:23.

My gut flopped with panic.

Crap! Nancy Meyers will have my hide!

Nancy Meyers lived directly across the street from me. As the self-appointed Neighborhood Yard Sale Captain, Nancy ran the annual event with military precision. According to the strict regulations spelled out in her Yard Sale Code of Conduct pamphlet, in order to qualify to participate in the event, my table had to be stocked and ready for her inspection no later than 7:45 a.m.

Crap! I just wasted eight full minutes setting up the table!

Nancy Meyers was a neighborhood legend well before I moved to Bahia Shores. Since she'd arrived from the motherland, she'd made it her business to know *everyone else's* business. A control freak could only aspire to such greatness.

From the neighborhood yard sale to lawn maintenance to dog poop compliance, Nancy wielded her dictatorial hand over every move her neighbors made, gathering her intel by peering at us through binoculars from her living room window.

Over the years, Nancy's anal-retentive antics had earned her a few nicknames. People of a certain age called her Mrs. Kravitz' crazy cousin. Others, Bristol-Butt Meyers. But my favorite moniker for her was the Knick-Knack Nazi.

Middle-aged and with a sphincter tight enough to poop diamonds, Nancy was purportedly married to a guy named Ralph. I'd never seen him, personally. No one had. Rumor had it she kept him chained up in a cage in their basement. But I knew that was preposterous. Florida's water table was too shallow to allow for a basement.

On the advice of seasoned residents, I'd made it a point to keep my distance from Nancy. She was definitely someone I didn't want to cross.

Even though I didn't care much for her arbitrary, nit-picking deadline, I followed along for two reasons.

For one, it got me out of doing the breakfast dishes. Secondly, and much more importantly, the 7:45 a.m. "curfew" enabled me to get first crack at the merchandise my neighbors were hawking *before* the general public swooped in at eight o'clock.

Like the old saying goes, "The early bird gets the worm." But then again, worms weren't exactly what I was after.

As I walked down the drive, I mopped the sweat dripping from my brow with the green tablecloth in my hand. I flung the waterlogged square of material over the folding table. Across the street, a stout, blonde woman in a military-green shift-dress gave me a disapproving look. I fiddled with the tablecloth until it was centered, tidy, and Nancy's lips unsnarled.

Another glance down at my cellphone told me I had nineteen minutes to haul out any junk I wanted to sell. I turned to head back into the garage to gather up my yard sale stuff. As I did, I took a peek down the street at the rest of the homes lining Bimini Circle.

I gasped.

In front of nearly every house, folding tables laden with junk lined the sidewalks and spilled out into the grass...*and my neighbors were already going through them!*

Nooooo!

I abandoned my empty table and sprinted over to my neighbor Jake's place. To my surprise, his table looked more like a trade-show booth than a yard sale jumble. Lined up in neat rows were various dog-training paraphernalia, along with cards and mugs and flyers advertising his dog-psychology business, You're In Charge.

Jake the ape-man wasn't around, so I scrambled over to the neighbor to his left...and then the neighbor after that one.

I should have known better.

I was only three tables in, and already I'd seen at least a half-dozen sappy figurines, including two sad-eyed hound dogs, two goofy golfers, a chubby pizza baker and a woefully mislabeled "World's Greatest Dad."

Everywhere I looked, insipid figurines stared back at me, begging to be put out of their misery by my Hammer of Justice.

My upper lip twitched. Rabid, unquenched desire surged through my veins. Overwhelmed by temptation, I felt as frustrated as a klepto-maniac with no thumbs.

What was I thinking? Why on Earth *had I made that stupid deal with Tom? Why?!?*

As if to pour salt in my psychological wounds, staring back at me from the table in front of me was another atrocity of the ceramic kind. It was a planter in the shape of a sad-sack clown. A thumb-sized cactus stuck strategically from the front of its drooping pants.

The fingernails on my hammer hand dug into my palm.

I'm at a freaking plaster-of-Paris buffet...with duct tape across my mouth!

"Val Fremden!"

The high-pitched, nasal voice behind me made my back arch like a startled cat.

I whirled around.

Three doors down, across the street from my house, a pair of binoc-ulars were trained on me. Knick Knack Nancy waved with the clip-board in her hand.

"Are you ready?" she yelled and poked the clipboard in the direc-tion of my house. "It's 7:37!"

"No, ma'am!" I hollered back like a wayward soldier. "But I'll get right to it!"

I gave the pornographic cactus man one last dirty look and made a beeline for my garage.

MY HANDS TREMBLED AS I lined up Tom's old potato peeler alongside Tom's old Mr. Coffee machine and Tom's old stereo speakers. Across the street, Nancy was standing at attention in front of her own table of junk, ticking off items on her clipboard. I supposed she must have been giving *herself* an inspection.

It wouldn't have surprised me.

But I had to hand it to her. Nancy had thrown me a morsel of kindness. For some reason, she'd left the inspection of my table for last. Either she was giving me more time, or she was saving me for dessert after making a meal out of the rest of the neighbors.

I looked up from placing Tom's old wooden spoons next to Tom's old football. Nancy was marching across the street toward me, tapping a pen on her clipboard. It was 7:44 a.m., on the dot.

My hour of reckoning was at hand.

I gulped and scrambled for the last box on the ground beside me. One of Nancy's cardinal yard-sale rules read that if an item wasn't on the sale table at the time of her inspection, it could not, under any circumstances, be added later.

I hoisted up the last box of junk beside my table just as the Knick Knack Nazi's heels touched my driveway. I hastily dumped its contents onto the table. Out tumbled an assortment of crap, including an old hairbrush, a chipped coffee cup, and an object I'd never seen before.

As if on cue, the purple, bullet-shaped apparatus rolled to the front of the table and saluted Nancy's navel as she arrived.

Nancy glanced disdainfully at the item and cleared her throat.

"Regulations ban the sale of...ahem...*personal* items, Fremden. I suggest you put that 'thing' back where it came from."

"Yes, ma'am."

My face grew as red-hot as a baboon's behind. I grabbed the blasted 'thing' off the table. Tom must have put it there as another one of his stupid jokes of late. Then my mind squirmed to a less pleasant thought.

OMG! Maybe the thing belonged to an old girlfriend of his!

I tossed the six-inch purple bullet back into the empty box and contemplated where Tom could stick his "personal item."

"It won't happen again, Nancy," I said.

"See that it doesn't."

Nancy frowned at her clipboard, then sighed. "Okay. I guess you're good to go."

"Thank you, ma'am."

Nancy turned on her heels and headed back toward her house. "But you're on thin ice, Fremden," she shot as she walked away. "I'll have my eye on you."

I saluted Nancy behind her back, then carried the box back inside the garage. I thought about Tom and his practical joke. It deserved an elaborate payback. But I didn't have time at the moment to cook up a scheme. So, I decided to let sleeping vibrators lie.

For now.

Chapter Seven

It was 7:56 a.m. and I was ready for duty as a full-fledged, Nancy-Meyers-certified participant of the Annual Bahia Shores Yard Sale and Bake-Off.

Let the festivities begin.

I stood at attention behind my table laden with Tom's used household wares. Across the street, Nancy herself gave me a quick nod of approval. As I nodded back, something on the Knick-Knack Nazi's table caught my eye.

I did a double-take. Then a triple.

I still couldn't believe my eyes.

It was...impossible!

I grabbed Tom's old bifocals off the table and gave the object a fourth look. Either I was hallucinating from the heat, or someone needed to be imprisoned for crimes against humanity.

Either way, I was at my wits' end.

I glanced down the street. A hoard of shoppers was assembling, bulging like a pregnant termite queen's belly against the rope cordoning off the street. No one could gain access to the sale until the Knick Knack Nazi had given her official approval.

Seizing my narrow window of opportunity, I abandoned my post, went AWOL, and made a mad dash across the street.

The closer I got to Nancy's yard sale table, the more I realized it hadn't been a mirage brought on by sudden figurine withdrawal. Not even *my* imagination was that twisted.

I blinked back my astonishment. There, tucked between an old toaster and a stack of curling paperbacks, was the most hideous thing I'd ever laid eyes on.

From the depths of some deviant's rotten mind had come the tacky figurine to beat *all* tacky figurines.

My mouth went slack with shock and awe as I stared at the eight-inch high, life-like statuette of a morbidly obese, shirtless man. The barrel-bellied guy was perched on a toilet, his pudgy hands gripping either side of the seat.

His stomach hung over his privates and covered his legs almost to his knees. A pair of red-and-white polka-dotted boxers were wadded in a heap at his ankles. Tiny beads of sweat trailed down his shiny, bald head, past a jowly face with squinting eyes and a grimacing mouth.

The inscription on the base below his bare feet was the icing on the crap-cake.

"I hope everything works its way out for you."

My upper lip twitched involuntarily. My fingers began to fidget. I swallowed the twin pools of drool that had accumulated on either side of my tongue. My seething mind was blank, save for one lone, throbbing thought:

Doo-Doo Daddy must die.

"How much for the figurine?" I asked Nancy, then coughed nervously.

Nancy looked up from her clipboard. "Against regulations. No resales, Fremden. Get back to your post!"

A twinge of something akin to hysteria shot through me. "Re...*resales?*" I stuttered.

Nancy looked down her piggish nose at me. "Haven't you read the guidelines? You can't buy something from me, then sell it again at your table."

"I...I wasn't planning on reselling it."

Nancy eyed me dubiously. Her snout crinkled.

"You weren't?"

"No, ma'am. What gave you *that* idea?"

"I figured...well...I mean, what on Earth would you want...." Nancy glanced up the street toward the gathering crowd, then back at me. "Listen, Val. I know times are tough, but *really!*"

"Huh? What are you talking about?"

"Well, I didn't want to say anything, but rumor has it you quit your job and...well...you could use the money."

"Who told you *that?*"

Nancy shrugged defensively. "I dunno. The grapevine, I guess."

"Really? Who's swinging from it?"

Nancy scowled. "Listen, it's against regulations to –"

"Just gimme a hint," I said, cutting her off. "Was it a *Tarzan* or a *Jane?*"

Nancy checked her Swiss watch. "Look, Fremden. It's 7:58.47. I've gotta go and put on my money belt."

"Give me the figurine, and I'll leave you to it."

Nancy sighed. "Okay. Five bucks."

"Five bucks? For *that thing?* That's outrageous!"

Nancy smiled like a sneaky dog. She glanced down the road again. Cars were lining up along the street. People were piling out and dragging little wheeled shopping carts behind them. She shrugged.

"Take it or leave it, Fremden. It's your call."

I thought about it for a split second. Five bucks to rid the world of that hideous stink bomb? The thought of my hammer obliterating that slob's grimacing face was too much to resist.

"Okay. I'll go get the money."

I reached for the figurine. Nancy snatched it off the table and smirked evilly.

"Let's see the cash first."

My mouth fell open. "What? You don't trust me?"

Nancy's nearly lipless slit of a mouth twisted cruelly. "Desperate people do desperate things."

"You think I'm *desperate?*"

Nancy shrugged and looked up at the heavens. "It's not what *I* think that matters."

I turned and ran back across the street to my house, trying not to crack my gnashing teeth. I flung open the door, skittered into the kitchen and grabbed my purse off the counter.

"What's up?" Tom asked, looking up from the sink.

"I need five dollars," I said as I fished out my wallet.

Tom's left eyebrow arched. "What for?"

"For a ffff..."

My voice fizzled out like a dying balloon. My gut punched itself as I scrambled for a white lie. Preferably one that began with an "F."

"For...*funds*. You know. *Change*," I bumbled. "Nancy across the street...she's going to give me change. For, you know, yard sale customers and stuff."

I set my face to stone mode and studied Tom's expression. Had he bought my bag of baloney?

He smiled, picked up a plate from the drain board and began to dry it with a dishtowel. "Okay."

My lips pursed with guilt...or something like it. But I had no time for true confessions. I ran out the door with my wallet, wondering who the bigger shmuck was, me or Tom.

A few footsteps out the door, I stopped in my tracks. Nancy wasn't at her table. *And neither was my figurine!*

I scurried to her door and banged on it like a junkie on a bender. Nancy opened the door, scowled, and put her hands on her hips. Slung around her waist like a Wild-West gun holster was what looked to be a coin-operated chastity belt.

Lucky Ralph.

"Uh...here's your five bucks," I stuttered. "Gimme the figurine."

"Geeze, Fremden. Your upper lip is sweating. Are you okay?"

"Uh...sure. Come on. Hand it over!"

Nancy tucked the fiver in her utility belt and handed me the crappy figurine. I snatched it from her hand, took a step toward home, then realized I couldn't let Tom see me with my ceramic contraband.

"Uh...look, Nancy. Could you just keep it for me...until the end of the day?"

She eyed me suspiciously.

"I guess so. Why?"

"I don't want it, you know, to get mixed up with my own yard sale stuff...and, you know, commit an accidental *resale*."

Nancy nodded and took the figurine back. "Yes. Of course. I'll file it away on the 'F' shelf in my garage."

Alphabetized garage shelves? You gotta be kidding me!

"Thank you, Nancy. Now, I'd better get back to my own table."

"Hop to it," Nancy barked. She looked over my shoulder and her face suddenly softened into something resembling a human expression.

"Hi, Tom!" she called and waved.

The hair on the back of my neck stood up. I turned around. Tom was outside, perusing the merchandise on our table.

Crap on a cracker!

He looked up and waved back. "Morning!" he called out. "Great weather for the sale."

I angled my torso to hide the clandestine figurine still in Nancy's clutches.

"Yes, it sure is," Nancy cooed sweetly. "I hope you take time to enjoy your day, Tom! Don't forget to stop and smell the roses!"

I nearly stumbled over my own two feet.

I'd have been more prepared for a locust plague than for Nancy's transformation from battle-axe to sweetheart. In my humble opinion, it sounded as if Nancy Meyers was a little too pleased to see Tom – and I was none too pleased about it myself.

"Well, here come the hoards," I said, eyeing Nancy with new eyes. "I guess we should all get busy."

"Right," Nancy said, switching back to battalion mode. "Wait a second. Did you contribute to the bake off, Fremden? I didn't see anything with your name on it at the baked goods table."

"I plan to," I said sourly. "I just haven't gotten around to it yet."

Nancy's thin lips tried to purse, but just made a white line under her nose.

"What are you waiting for, Fremden?" she barked.

"Uh...a *friend*."

"Who?"

"Confidentiality regulations restrict my ability to outsource that information," I said.

"Oh. Of course," Nancy replied.

She looked back across the street at Tom and smiled, as unfazed by my jabbing punch at her regulatory tomfoolery as a seasoned prize-fighter with an inch-thick skull.

Chapter Eight

"I'll give you this wooden spoon and the toothpick holder for that figurine," I said to the old lady.

Like a desperate camel stumbling alone in the Sahara, I'd spotted the ceramic oasis in her clutches as soon as she'd hobbled within ten feet of me.

"This thing?" she asked, and glanced down at the object in her hand.

It was a statuette of a portly, round-bottomed woman with an exaggerated neck that stretched high above her, giving her the overall shape of a Chianti bottle.

The old woman gripped the figurine by its elongated throat, as if she were throttling it. I was jonesing to do the hideous figurine one better.

"Yeah, that thing," I answered. "Lemme see it."

She set the figurine on my yard-sale table. Only when she released her gnarled fingers did the extent of the waste of perfectly good porcelain become fully apparent.

The pear-bottomed figure was clad in a brown-and-gold, animal-print unitard that spanned the length of her impossibly long neck, and formed a tight hoodie all the way to her forehead. On top of her head were two short antennae and pointy, cat-like ears. Inscribed on the base below her hooved feet was a pun so bad it made me groan out loud.

Gee Your Affable.

Never before had three little words been used so effectively to devastate both art and literature simultaneously.

I picked up the abomination and glared into its miniscule, beady eyes. "Giraffe woman" stared back, begging me to put her out of her illiterate misery. It was my civic duty to oblige.

"The toothpick holder and the spoon," I offered again. "Whatta you say?"

The old woman's sharp eyes scanned my table.

"Throw in that bottle opener there and you got yourself a deal," she said.

I looked around to make sure Tom wasn't nosing about, and gave the woman a quick nod.

"Deal."

I stuffed the kitchen gadgets into the old lady's bag, then quickly tucked the Abominable Giraffe Woman into a box, along with Turtle Boy, another figurine I'd traded for Tom's old football. I stole a glance across the street. The Knick Knack Nazi was giving me the stank-eye.

Too bad.

I waved and smiled. "No resale," I yelled.

Nancy scowled and tilted her head in a way that made me feel she wasn't buying it. But I didn't care. It wasn't a lie. Reselling those figurines was totally off the table. Not only would it have been against yard-sale regulations – it would have been against basic human decency.

"Good doing business with you," I said to the old woman.

"You, too, hun."

"Have a nice day," I added, and turned to stash my box of ill-gotten ceramics on a shelf in the garage.

"Not likely in today's litigious society," a man's voice sounded behind me. "Here. Take one of my cards."

I turned to see a tall, skinny man wearing a Hawaiian shirt and baggy shorts. A ludicrously large pair of pink, heart-shaped sunglasses sat atop his angular, pointy nose, which protruded from under the sunglasses like an anemic beak. A thin cloud of curly, reddish-brown frizz topped his pasty white noggin.

As he extended a long, wimpy arm toward the old lady, a flicker of recognition sent a jolt of disgust through my gut.

"Ferrol Finkerman," I hissed under my breath.

I glared at the opportunistic attorney who'd twice tried to extort money from me with false claims. Once for human finger dismemberment, the other for indecent toupee exposure.

Finkerman patted the old lady's shoulder dismissively and looked over at me. One look at his hideous smile made me grit my teeth and wish I'd filed a restraining order against the clod when I'd had the chance.

"Well, if it isn't Ms. Fremden in the flesh," he said, then folded his arms and stared at me through those dumb glasses like a half-plucked ostrich that'd just won the booby prize at a roadside carnival.

"What are *you* doing here?" I spat.

"Can't a man have his leisure activities?" he asked jovially.

My lips pursed as I tried to hold in the distasteful thoughts welling up in my throat.

"What's with the stupid glasses?" I said sourly.

"These? Just picked 'em up at one of the tables. You know, in my line of work, it pays to go incognito. Unrecognizable is unidentifiable...in a court of law, if you catch my drift."

"Too bad you're not wearing something big enough to cover up your sleaze."

Finkerman's eyebrow arched high enough to clear the oversized glasses.

"Ouch," he smirked, and glanced around at the junk on my table. "Got any old library books for sale?"

"What? No. Why?"

Finkerman smiled. I immediately thought of my Aunt Pansy. She'd once told me that a smile could improve *anyone's* appearance. But I guess that theory only worked for human beings.

"It's a hobby of mine," Finkerman said. "A little public service, if you will."

I snorted. "Public service? Don't make me laugh, Finkerman. What's your angle?"

Finkerman's lips twisted and puckered into a puffy lump.

"You know me so well, Val. I like that about you."

He leaned over the table toward me and whispered, making the nasal tone of his voice somehow even more annoying.

"In my spare time, I send notices to people who fail to return library books. Here. I'll show you."

Finkerman took a book from his bag of yard-sale finds and opened it to the back cover. He pulled the lending card from its paper pocket, studied it, and shook his head.

"Tsk. Tsk. Tsk. It seems Manny Delrose was supposed to return this book on or before March 30th, 1998. He didn't, and now it's time to pay the piper, Mr. Melrose."

"What are you talking about, Finkerman?"

The pasty-faced attorney looked up at me and spoke as if he were quoting sing-song rhymes from a Dr. Seuss book. "Well, it appears a fine is in need. Yes, a fine would be fine. Oh yes, fine indeed."

I crossed my arms. "A *fine?* What do you mean? Don't tell me you're.... No way! You're not...*working for the library*, are you?"

Finkerman threw back his head and laughed, revealing a jumble of piranha teeth.

"Ha ha! Of course not! The state doesn't pay squat, Fremden! Besides, I don't need *them*."

"So, what are you talking about?"

Finkerman slipped the lending card back into its pocket, closed the book and held it up as if he were going to give a lecture on his new USA

Today award-winning novel. If the title had been *How to Be a Disgusting Weasel*, he'd have nailed it.

"I'm talking about sending Manny a letter from my law office mentioning the tardy nature of said book. Along with, of course, an offer to keep Mr. Delrose from garnering a criminal record for theft of public property. Believe it or not, a simple letter like that can earn me a tidy sum."

I shook my head in disgust.

"That's *sick*, Finkerman. Even for you. I wouldn't think a book fine would be worth your precious time."

"That's just it, Fremden. It takes no time at all. I've got it all down to a simple form letter. Insert name and address. Mail it off. Two minutes work, tops. Not a bad way to earn $89.94."

My eyebrows collided. "What?"

Finkerman grinned slyly. "That's the threshold people will pay to make a legal problem go away...*without* court dates, legal repercussions, and, most importantly, no pesky questions being asked."

My nose crinkled. "How do you *know* that? Ugh! Never mind."

Finkerman's grin was giving me the willies.

"Hey, guilty consciences are what make the world go round, Fremden. People are so gullible, they'll fall for all kinds of scams."

"So!" I said, and pointed a finger at him. "You admit that what you're doing's a *scam!*"

Finkerman's spine straightened. "You aren't recording this, are you?"

I slumped from disappointment at the missed opportunity. "No. Are you?"

Finkerman touched a square-shaped lump in his breast pocket. "So...I never said the word 'scam.' Capeesh?"

I rolled my eyes. "Whatever."

Finkerman cleared his throat. "On another note, you wouldn't happen to be thinking of suing anyone, would you?"

My jaw nearly hit the sidewalk. "You must *really* be hard up to be asking *me* that, Finkerman."

"Why?"

"Because when I think of dirtbags, only one person comes to mind."

He laughed. "Oh, come on, Val. I thought we were old pals."

"Pals?!" I snorted. "You must be crazy! Who would want to be pals with *you?*"

Finkerman shrugged. "In my book, a pal is anyone who isn't actively plotting my demise."

I shook my head. "I bet *that's* a short list."

I was about to tell the ambulance chaser to beat it when something stopped me cold. A figurine was poking its head out of his bag of books.

"What's that?" I asked.

"This thing?"

Finkerman plucked the little statue from his bag. It was an Asian-looking woman standing with a gavel in one hand, a briefcase in the other. Her name was Su Mee.

"Charming, isn't she?" Finkerman asked.

Compared to *him*, yes. And after the slimy conversation I'd just had about attorneys abusing the law, I wanted Su Mee something fierce.

"I'll trade you a Mr. Coffee machine for the statue thing," I said, trying to sound casual.

Finkerman studied the statue as if it were made of gold and precious gems. "Sorry. No can do."

I blew out a breath. "Come on, Finkerman. What do you want for it?"

Finkerman surveyed my table of used household crap and stuck up his pointy nose. Then he looked past me into the garage. His upper lip curled like the corner of a soggy affidavit.

"That tray of cookies behind you," he said.

I turned around and glanced at the heaping pile of snickerdoodles. I'd baked a double batch last night.

"I dunno...."

"Come on, Fremden. It's just the thing I need to impress a new client tomorrow. You know, something home baked. It could give me that... what do you call it? 'Illusion of humanity.'"

It would've taken a lot more than cookies to convince me Finkerman was human. But who was I to argue? I wanted to rid the world of Su Mee something awful. I grabbed the figurine from his pale, boney fingers.

"Deal," I said, and stuffed the statuette in the box with the others. I hoisted the tray of cookies from the shelf and handed it to him.

"Nice doing business with you again, *pal*," Finkerman sneered. "That figurine set me back a whole seventy-five cents. Ha ha! *I win!*"

As I watched Finkerman disappear down the sidewalk with his prize, the door that led from the house into the garage opened. Tom came out and gave me a kiss and a cool glass of water.

"Whew!" he exclaimed. "It's hot as blazes! How're you doing?"

"Okay. How about you?"

"I tell you what, Val, those are some pretty tough old gals manning that bake sale table. It wasn't easy, but the switch is done."

"Good work."

Tom glanced over at the garage shelf. "Hey. What'd you do with Laverne's cookies?"

A satisfied smile curled my lips.

"Don't worry, Tom. I donated them to a very good cause."

Chapter Nine

"I still don't understand how we only made four dollars and thirty-seven cents for all my old stuff," Tom said as I counted the money out into his palm.

I shrugged. "Times are tough. Nobody pays much for used junk anymore. Look on the bright side. At least the garage is almost cleaned out. And we've still got tomorrow to make your fortune."

Tom shook his head. "I hope you know what this means."

"What?"

"You can never, ever break up with me, Val Fremden. I could never afford to buy all that stuff again."

I smirked. "Well, there's always next year's yard sale. If need be, maybe you can recoup it all."

Tom grinned and shook his head. "Anyone ever tell you you've got an evil streak?"

I batted my lashes at him. "Oh...at least once a day."

Tom laughed. "You're incorrigible."

I pouted. "That's not very nice."

Tom wrapped his arms around me. "Oh, come on, Val. Incorrigibility is the thing I love most about you."

While I decided on my mood, Tom kissed me on the nose.

"By the way," he added, "let me know when you're done with the sale tomorrow and I'll haul the rest of the boxes out to the street for the garbage men."

"Okay," I said. "By the way, that's *my* favorite thing about *you*."

"What?"

"That you take care of the garbage."

"Nice to know I'm appreciated for my talents, smarty pants."

Tom released me from his arms and jingled the change in his hand.

"So, how do you want to blow our winnings?" he asked.

I took him by the arm and gave him a coy grin.

"It's Saturday night. I'm sure a handsome man like you can think of something."

SUNDAY MORNING, WHILE Tom was in the shower, I bolted for the garage. I needed to get the yard sale table in order before I got nailed by the Knick Knack Nazi. I also needed to get my contraband figurines out of the garage before Tom took out the trash. I'd smuggled Doo-Doo Daddy home last night after the sale. He was now with the other three figurines hiding out like illegal immigrants in a box in my garage....

As my fingers wrapped around the doorknob leading out to the garage, my cellphone buzzed. I jumped as if the blasted door handle had been electrified.

The display on my cellphone read: *Scam Likely*. I stepped into the garage, hit the door opener and answered the call anyway.

"Hello?"

"I can't believe you poisoned me!" a man's trembling voice hissed. "I thought we were pals!"

"Finkerman?"

"Who else? Or do you make a *habit* of poisoning people?"

"It was the word 'pals' that threw me off," I said. "I never agreed to that. Anyway, what are you talking about?"

"Those cookies. What was in them?"

"Uh...what?"

"You heard me. Do we need to go to the emergency room, or is this survivable?"

"*We?*"

"Me and my...*client.*"

"Since when do you see clients on Sunday?"

"Okay. It was *a date.* You satisfied?"

I stifled a snort. "Sure. Was *she?*"

"Har har. Now cut the crap and answer the question, Fremden. Do I need to call poison control? Take ipecac? Get my stomach pumped in the ER?"

"Describe your symptoms."

Finkerman growled. "I could sue you, you know."

"Really? For what?"

"Assault with a deadly cookie."

"I didn't *force* you eat them, Finkerman. Besides, *you're* the one who wanted the snickerdoodles in the first place. As I recall, it was *you* who initiated the trade. You even proclaimed you'd *won.*"

"Irrelevant! Probably.... Anyway, I can still get you for intent to do bodily harm."

"I don't think so. You see, I didn't *make* the cookies, Finkerman. So how was *I* to know they would cause you...*stomach distress.*"

"Aha! You *knew*, all right! Those cookies were gastric time bombs! I'll have you know I crapped my pants – in my Hummer – driving down U.S. 19!"

I stifled a laugh and imagined the cover of my first mystery novel featuring a yellow Hummer on the cover...*Dial "D" for Diarrhea....*

"So?" I snorted. "What do you want *me* to do about it?"

"I'm at Walmart now, buying new underpants."

I clenched my jaw against the rising need to laugh out loud.

"Geeze, Finkerman. That must be...uh...*embarrassing.*"

"Not really," Finkerman said dryly. "Like I said, I'm at *Walmart.*"

"Look," I said. "How about this? I'll pay for your underwear, and even throw in an air freshener for your Hummer."

"Aha! So, you *admit* your guilt. Thanks. That's all I need for now."

The phone clicked off. I stared at the blank screen. A niggling thread of dread began to gnaw away at my gut.

"Oh, crap. What have I done?"

"What's wrong, sugar?" Laverne's voice sounded nearby.

I looked up. My bobble-headed neighbor was smiling at me like a kindly mother donkey.

"You know that old saying, Laverne? 'No good deed goes unpunished?'"

"Yeah."

"You're looking at its latest victim."

Laverne's bulgy eyes went puppy-dog sad. "What was your good deed, honey?"

I smirked sourly.

"I saved the world from your deadly...."

Oh, crap!

"...uh...*figurines*." I grabbed the box off the shelf and showed her my motley collection.

Laverne peeked inside the box. "But, sugar, those aren't *mine*."

I chewed my lip, grateful Laverne's one-gear mind hadn't picked up on the word "deadly."

"Are you *sure*, Laverne?"

Laverne peered into the box again and nodded sternly.

"Oh, yes. I'm sure, honey. I used to collect those Dr. Dingbat figures. But I gave them up. You know, J.D. says they're too crude."

"Dr. Dingbat?"

Laverne reached into the box and plucked out the figurine of the fat man on the toilet. She flipped it over, exposing two unsightly brown bottoms.

"See here? This one's called, Diagnosis: Difficult Defecation."

My upper lip jerked as if it'd been caught on a fishhook.

"You don't say, Laverne."

"No. I don't. The figurine does, Val. Right here."

Laverne pointed a red-lacquered nail at the words embossed into the ceramic figure's posterior. "See that double 'D' there? That makes it a genuine Dr. Dingbat."

"How do you *know* that, Laverne?"

"Well, as another old sayin' goes, Val, 'It takes one to know one.'"

I couldn't argue with that.

WHILE TOM WAS AWAY at the gas station filling his SUV, I seized the opportunity to smuggle my ill-gotten loot over the border from my garage into the house.

A criminal thrill raced through me as I transferred each forbidden figurine into an awaiting shoebox, then snuck across the threshold of the garage door and back into the house.

Evading the watchful eye of the border cop, I safely stowed the tacky collection away in the back of my closet, right between a shoebox full of Halloween candy and box containing a pair of high heels I knew I'd never wear, but, nevertheless, couldn't foresee a future worth living without.

As I slid the box of contraband ceramics into place, a sigh of relief escaped my lips. I tried to convince myself that I wasn't officially cheating on my deal with Tom. After all, I'd only *procured* them. Technically, no figurines had been smashed...yet.

The way I saw it, I was simply preparing for the day when I could exercise the glaring loophole in Tom's wager. He hadn't said I had to give up figurines *forever*. Just for four weeks. If I could hold out that long, he'd get rid of his hideous chair, and I could go back to my penchant for pulverizing porcelain.

And this new batch of mutant miscreations would do nicely.

I closed the closet door and chewed my bottom lip.

All I have to do now is keep my mitts off them for a month.

Failing that, I suppose I could always buy a slipcover for Tom's chair....

Chapter Ten

It was 7:57 a.m. Sunday morning and both I and my yard-sale table were again up and ready for action. Across the street, Knick Knack Nancy was peering down the street with her binoculars. I couldn't stand the suspense, so I walked over to investigate.

"What are you looking at?" I asked.

Nancy lowered her binoculars, revealing a face perpetually frozen with annoyance.

"Surveying the troops," she said.

She nodded toward the bake sale table at the end of the block, and poked the spyglass back in front of her ice-water-blue peepers. She grunted and shook her head.

"Ugh," she groaned. "Can you believe it? Connors is bringing the same thing she brought last year. I hope there's no raisins in it this time. Ugh! A Jello mold? Really, Gaylord? Who brings Jello to a bake sale? A cheapskate, that's who!"

Nancy dropped the binoculars and gave me the once over.

"What did *you* bring?" she demanded.

"Uh...snickerdoodles," I said. "A double batch!" I offered brightly, hoping to win favor with her, but losing some with my self-respect in the process.

"Ugh," Nancy grunted. "Same as Laverne. You two should coordinate your strategies better." She peeked through the binoculars again. "I only see one tray of snickerdoodles."

"Uh...yeah. I dropped mine and had to ditch them," I lied.

Nancy nearly dropped her spy wear. "That's pathetic, Fremden! If it were up to me, you'd be demoted to peeling potatoes."

I let that one slide, since I no longer owned a potato peeler.

"What did *you* bring, Nancy?"

It was a fair question, but one I knew Nancy was always loath to answer. As secretive as she was stodgy, Nancy always postponed revealing her bake-off entry until Sunday. Nobody knew why. Maybe she was hoping to win a medal of honor for it. Maybe she was just nuts.

"I made my double-fudge brownies," she said proudly. "They're famous in Stuttgart. Now, off to your post, Fremden. And take the clipboard with you. We might as well get the voting started."

I nodded in lieu of a formal salute, and headed back across the street. As I reached the sidewalk, I glanced down the road. Over by the bake sale table, one of the ladies was releasing the rope that cordoned off the customers. A throng of rabid-looking yard-sale enthusiasts started pouring into the street.

"You ready?" Jake called to me from his stand next door.

"I guess so," I called back, and took a quick detour over toward his table. Halfway through his yard, I stepped in a hole and fell to one knee on the grass.

"What the heck?" I called out.

"Sorry," Jake said. "Post hole. Some jerk took my sign again."

I glanced back toward Nancy. She quickly looked away. "I think I have an idea who."

"Tell me!" Jake said.

I leaned over the table and whispered in his hairy ear. "It's brownies. Spread the word."

"Brownies? Who the heck is brownies?"

I'd forgotten Jake was new to the neighborhood. "The bake off. The Knick Knack Nazi made brownies. Vote for her and she has to kiss that pig."

"Huh? Why would I want to make that poor pig kiss a Nazi?"

"Oh. Sorry. Not a Nazi. *Nancy.*" I nodded toward Nancy's place. "That's her...uh...nickname."

Jake looked over at Nancy. "Why?"

"Well, for a few reasons. Listen, I can't say for certain, Jake, but I'm like...one hundred and fifty percent sure Nancy's the one who's been taking your signs."

This time, Jake's eyes looked different as they shifted their gaze across the street to where Brunhilda was busy polishing her knick-knacks.

"Why would she do that?" he asked.

I shrugged. "Sadistic pleasure?"

Jake grimaced. "Geeze."

He shot a glance down the street toward the bake sale. I figured he was either trying to get a look at Nancy's brownies or the little pink piglet frolicking in the grassy area by the baked goods table.

"So, what's it gonna be?" I asked. "Vote for the brownies and Nancy locks lips with a pig."

Jake grimaced. "I wouldn't wish that on any living creature."

I laughed. "Somebody's gotta do it. Anyway, you've got to vote for someone to win the bake-off. It's *tradition*, Jake. When you're done, pass the clipboard to the next table. They'll tally the votes at the end to decide the winner."

"Doesn't sound like winning to me," Jake muttered.

"Yeah. This year *is* kind of strange. Usually, the bake-off prize is something like a manicure or a grocery-store certificate. But this year...well, I dunno what happened."

Jake looked at the clipboard, his face sullen.

"Think of it Jake. For the first time in neighborhood yard sale history, we have a chance to stick it to the man...or should I say...to the *Knick Knack Nazi.*"

Jake studied me for a moment. "What have *you* got against her, Val?"

"Nothing anybody else in the neighborhood hasn't got. Listen, I've got to get back to my table. Just a friendly word of advice. Don't leave your garbage cans out past 8:30 in the morning or you'll get a nasty Nazi-gram."

Jake's hairy eyebrows slowly met and formed a small, swarthy mountain in the middle of his forehead.

"Don't tell me *she's* the one who left me that awful note."

"Uh...I'd bet good money on it."

Jake glanced over at Nancy, then back to me.

"Val, you don't think I resemble a *sloth*, do you?"

I bit my lip. "Of course not. Look Jake, I gotta go before Nancy fines me for loitering."

I shoved the clipboard into his hairy hand.

"Remember, vote for the brownies and we get to see Nancy kiss a pig!"

Jake shot me a devious grin. He grabbed the cheap ballpoint chained securely to the clipboard and said,

"Okay, Val. It's on."

Chapter Eleven

"Lord a-mighty, there's a carnage a people lollygaggin' 'round up in here," Winky commented as he strode up to my yard-sale table.

"What are *you* doing here?" I asked. "Shouldn't you be at your shop selling donuts or fishing worms or something?"

Winky glanced around as if to make sure nobody else was listening, then wagged his eyebrows at me.

"Winnie let me escape for an hour. I just couldn't bear missin' out on the yard sale of the century."

Winky's jovial expression sagged with disappointment as he looked over the meager offerings left on my table. Apparently, even *he* didn't want Tom's dented rice cooker with no lid or a used chia pet in the shape of a reclining gnome.

"Gaul dang it," Winky sulked. "I'm too late. Val, you done sold outta the good stuff."

"Sorry, Winky. How about a consolation prize? There's beer in the fridge."

Winky's frown did a backflip. "*Now* yore talkin'!"

I looked past his freckled face, down the sidewalk toward the crowd meandering my way.

"Go help yourself, Winky," I said, and hitched a thumb toward the garage. "I got customers coming."

As Winky disappeared into my house, a tiny, vestigial worm of anxiety wriggled in my gut. But I let it go. Now that Winky had Winnie and a home of his own, I wasn't nearly as worried whether he was house broken...or if he'd break my house.

I let go a breath and turned my attention to the man eyeing Tom's old stereo speakers. The wiry guy appeared to have more tattoos than teeth. Rice didn't require too many teeth to eat.

"You look like you need a rice cooker," I said to the toothless biker dude. "I'll let you have it for four bucks."

The guy sniffed. "I'll take it off your hands for a dollar."

"Deal."

He showed me his gums and picked up the rice cooker. "Where's my dollar?" he asked.

"What?"

"My dollar to take this thing off your hands."

I pictured Tom's rice cooker back in my kitchen, taking up precious cabinet space. If it was gone, so was that possibility.

I paid the guy a buck.

"And the gnome," he said.

I balked. "No way."

The biker dude laughed and shrugged. "Hey, it was worth a try."

"Good one," I said. "But it ain't gonna happen."

That gnome's made of terra-cotta, buddy. If nothing else, it's perfect target practice for my Hammer of Justice.

"Okay. Have a good one," he said and walked away.

"What in tarnation is this stuff?" Winky asked.

I whirled around to find the redheaded redneck riffling through a carton on a shelf in the garage. It was the box of discards for the sale. In it was Tom's purple *personal item!* I leapt to Winky's side and snatched the box out of his hands.

"Gimme that!"

Winky recoiled.

"Geeze, Val! Don't go all loony-toons on me! I was just lookin' for more stuff to fill out the sparse areas of yore table. Ain't you ever heard a merchandising?"

"No restocking!" I yelped. "It's the rules!"

Winky looked like he swallowed a wasp. "*Whose* rules?"

I looked toward the street. My hands were full holding the carton, so I jabbed my chin in that direction.

"*Hers.*"

Across the road, Nancy Meyers was swatting the hand of some kid who'd made the mistake of reaching for her used paperbacks.

"Believe me, Winky, you don't want to get on that woman's bad side."

"You're telling me she's got a *good* one?" Winky snorted. "From where I'm standin', she looks purty bad from every angle, if'n you ask me."

"Well I never!" said a woman walking up to my table. She stopped dead in her tracks, shot us both a dirty look, and huffed off toward Jake's place.

"Ma'am!" I called after her. "He wasn't talking about you!"

I stifled a grin and shook my head at Winky. He was funny, but bad for business. And I still had Tom's 1980s-era speakers and boom box to unload.

"Do me a favor, Winky," I said. "Go down and get me a brownie from the bake sale. And pick up one for yourself, if you want."

I pulled a dollar from my change purse and started to hand it to him, but he pushed it away.

"You forget, Val. I'm a man 'a means, now. I'll buy."

"You're right. Tell you what, why don't you do me a *different* favor. Watch the table for me, Winky. I'll run down there and get us both a brownie. And it'll give me a chance to get a better look at that pig."

"Okay," Winky shrugged. "But you're gonna have to get the binoculars away from her first."

I BOUGHT TWO BROWNIES, petted the cute little pink pig, and skedaddled back before Winky could do too much damage. On my way there, I saw Jake standing at Nancy's table, chatting her up. He handed her one of his shiny "You're In Charge" coffee mugs, then ambled back toward his own table.

A twinge of jealousy pinged around in my head like a stray BB pellet.

What is this mysterious power Nancy has over men? Jake never offered me a mug! Not that I'd really wanted one...but that's beside the point!

I marched past Winky over to Jake's table.

"What are you doing?" I demanded. "Cavorting with the enemy?"

Jake looked taken aback, then laughed. "Oh. It's not what you think, Val."

"What do you mean, not what I think?"

He shrugged like a bored chimp. "You know the old saying, 'What goes around comes around.'"

"Yeah. So?"

I picked up a mug from his table and sulked.

"Why'd you give *her* one of these?"

"Strategic tactic," he said, and tapped a hairy finger on his bald noggin. "A little thing I like to call 'phonetic justice.'"

Jake's elusory wordplay was getting on my last nerve. I slammed the mug down on his table.

"Like I said before, Jake. I don't get it."

"*You're in* Charge, Val," he said, and looked at me as if his meaning should be perfectly obvious now.

I picked up the mug and raised it in preparation to bean Jake on the head with it.

He got the hint.

Jake held his hands up in a kind of defensive surrender, and continued his explanation.

"Okay, okay. Take it easy, Val. Look at it this way. Let's just say I 'charged' Nancy's coffee with a little urine...as in '*urine charge*.'"

I nearly swallowed my tongue. "You didn't."

Jake wagged his gorilla eyebrows. "I did."

"Jake, that's diabolical!"

He shrugged and studied the harry knuckles of his right hand.

"Eh. Not really. Just a little trick I picked up from my clients."

"Which ones?" I asked. "The canines or the criminals?"

Jake laughed. "Maybe a little of both."

I grimaced and looked back across the street just in time to see Nancy take a slug from the mug. I turned back to face Jake.

"Remind me not to get on *your* bad side."

Jake grinned sweetly and struck a pose, sort of like a contemplative gibbon.

"As anyone can see, Val, I don't have a bad side."

Chapter Twelve

Nancy raised her "You're In Charge" mug to her thin lips again. Part of me winced. Part of me cheered. And part of me scolded myself for not running over and knocking the cup from her hand.

As I walked back to my place, the train-wreck of a scene was so mesmerizing I failed to notice the other disaster unfolding at my own table.

"*There* you are," Winky hollered.

Startled, I nearly dropped the two brownies in paper napkins I held in my sweaty hands.

"Look who's here, Val!" Winky called out. "It's that feller what made me rich!"

I tore my eyes from *The Nancy Show* and zeroed in on Winky, then on the pasty, frizzy-headed jerk loitering around the chia pet and Tom's old boom box.

"Keep your hands off the merchandise," I warned Finkerman.

"This guy didn't make you rich, Winky. He just handled the paperwork."

I looked down at the stack of books in the shyster attorney's hand. "What'd you do, Finkerman? Break into the library's overnight book depository?"

Finkerman graced me with a toothy, insincere smile that reminded me of that shark in the old Star-Kist Tuna commercial.

"Very clever, Fremden. I'm just here to, as you said yourself, 'handle the paperwork.'"

Finkerman slapped an envelope in my hand.

"You've been served," he said, and did the shark-smile thing again.

"Served what?" Winky asked.

"A load of bull crap," I hissed, and glared at Finkerman.

"I what'n aware that bull crap came in envelopes," Winky said, and scratched his navel.

"The bull crap I'm talking about is outside the envelope," I said, my eyes locked on Finkerman.

Finkerman smirked. "Well then, my work here is done. I'll take my leave. Pleasure doing business with you, Fremden."

"The only pleasure in it for me is to see you go," I spat.

Finkerman tipped an imaginary hat. "Until we meet again. Very soon, I suspect."

My fingers crunched down on the envelope. "Until then, may you find a nice wood chipper to fall into, you pathetic, poisonous...*Pinocchio!*"

"What'n that thoughty a him, hand deliverin' yore mail 'n all," Winky said as Finkerman's frizzy head bobbed along amidst the crowd on the sidewalk. "But you got my curiosity up, Val. Why'd you call him Pinocchio? On account 'a his long nose?"

"No."

Winky scratched his chin. "'Cause he walks all kind a stove-up like?"

"No."

Winky picked up the chia gnome and studied it, as if it held the answer. "Well, why then?"

"Winky, I called him Pinocchio because, despite his appearance, Finkerman's not quite a real person."

Winky's eyes doubled in size.

"Naw! No foolin'? That there feller's one a them robot people I seen on TV?"

Winky shook his head in wonder. "Woo, doggy! Well, he sure fooled me!"

"Why doesn't that surprise me?" I muttered. "Put down the chia pet, Winky. Here's your brownie."

"Don't mind if I do. All this thankin's got me up an appetite somethin' fierce."

Winky set the chia gnome on my table, grabbed the brownie and took a bite out of it big enough to choke a Billy goat. He chewed once before his face went pale. Without warning, his mouth dropped opened and chunks of brown rubble tumbled out like peat moss from a derelict gumball machine.

"Good lord, Val! *Laverne* didn't make these thangs, did she?"

"No! I wouldn't do that to you!"

Winky held his hand to his throat and ran to the back of the garage. He grabbed his beer, took a slug, gargled with it, and spit out the dregs in the bushes on the side of the garage.

"Ugh! That was a close one," he said.

I eyed my brownie as if it were made of ground-up cockroaches. "Are they *really* that bad?"

Winky crinkled his freckled nose in disgust. "Let's just say, I've had gaul-dang *vegan food* that tasted better."

"Hey, you two!" Laverne called out as she made her way toward us in a flowery beach cover-up and six-inch silver heels.

My eyes shot a wary glance across the street at the Knick Knack Nazi.

"Laverne!" I said in a hushed tone. "What are you doing here? Who's manning your table?"

"Nobody, honey. I'm sold out!"

"How'd you manage that?" I asked.

"Well, sugar, it helps to add a little 'history' to your stuff. You know what I mean?"

"Uh...no," I said.

"Well, take that chia pet there," Laverne said. "Would you buy it if you knew it used to belong to..." she stopped and looked around, then whispered, "a *little person?*"

"You mean a midget?" Winky asked, his eyes growing wide.

"Yes," Laverne said.

Winky grabbed the chia pet and pawed at me, pleadingly. "How much you want for it, Val?"

"Wait a minute, Laverne," I said and turned my back to Winky. "All that stuff you sold was *J.D.'s?*"

Laverne grinned. "A girl's gotta do what a girl's gotta do. If all goes to plan, by next year's sale all he'll have left at my place is a weight bench in the garage."

"Respect," I whispered, and nearly curtseyed in admiration at the old woman who was clearly queen of her own Vegas-style domain.

Winky tugged on my sleeve. "Come on, Val! How much you want for the chia –"

"You can *have* it, Winky," I said.

Winky let out a hillbilly cheer. "Woo hoo! Boy howdy! Thanky, Val!"

He beamed at the ugly, worthless chia pet that had been made irresistible by Laverne's "historical embellishment." I had to hand it to her, Laverne had a hidden knack for showmanship.

"Did you get to see the little pig?" Laverne asked.

"Yeah," I answered. "Winky watched the table for me so I could go take a look. I'm curious, Laverne. Why would you want to kiss a pig, anyway?"

The skinny old woman shrugged her boney shoulders and laughed. "Just to see what it's like, I guess."

"It ain't *that* great," Winky said, and tucked the chia pet in a huge pocket on the left thigh of his cargo shorts.

"What?" I asked, the word escaping my mouth like a squeal. "How do *you* know?"

Winky shrugged.

"My cousin Thelma. She's spot on a match for that there little pig. 'Ceptin, a'course, that pig ain't got no moustache."

Chapter Thirteen

The time had come for someone to kiss a pig.

It was 5:00 p.m. on the dot, and the yard sale was officially over for the year. As the Knick Knack Nazi shooed malingering customers away with her police baton, the only thing left for the rest of us to do was fold up our tables and gather around for the official announcement of this year's bake-off winner.

Tom and I, along with Laverne and Jake, lined up around the pig's cage and waited as another neighbor, Doris Templeton, tallied the votes collected on Nancy's clipboard.

Jake eyed the piglet with sympathy. "Who in the world decided that the winner has to kiss that poor pig?"

"That kid over there suggested it," Tom said, and pointed to a young boy in a Cub Scout uniform. "He's raising the pig as part of his FFA project."

"FFA?" Jake asked.

"Future Farmers of America. Nancy told me she approved a pig as the prize, thinking it was going to be delivered as pork chops and bacon. But when the kid got wind of that, he broke down and cried."

"I didn't know you and Nancy were so close," I said, and eyed Tom up and down.

Tom shot me a sideways grin. "I wouldn't call it 'close.'"

"So what happens to the pig now?" Jake asked. "I mean, after the make-out session today?"

Tom shrugged. "I dunno. And to be perfectly honest, I don't *want* to know."

"Me either," I said.

"I think he'll go off to a farm in the country and make friends with a spider," Laverne offered brightly.

We all turned and stared at her.

"What?" she asked. "I read about it in a book."

Jake started to say something, but I cut him off.

"Yeah, Laverne," I said. "That's probably *exactly* what'll happen."

"Hush!" Nancy barked and waved her baton to silence the crowd. "Doris? Are you ready to announce the winner?"

Doris, a recent transplant from Ohio, cleared her throat and looked around nervously.

"Ahem...it seems as if we have...a *tie*."

She looked over at Nancy and smiled weakly. "It's between *your* brownies, Nancy, and...uh...Laverne's snickerdoodles."

I heard Laverne gasp.

"*Ein tie?*" Nancy bellowed. "*Das ist verboten!*"

She glared at our blank expressions with ice-water eyes. A moment later, she remembered she was in America, home of the free...and the English speaking. She pursed her thin, Germanic lips and grumbled at Doris.

"I mean, that's not allowed."

Nancy grabbed the clipboard from Doris' hands and studied it. Her accusatory eyes darted up, landed on a face in the crowd, then returned to the clipboard, then up at another face, then back to the clipboard. This continued for a minute or so as the crowd waited in dead silence for Nancy's verdict.

Suddenly, Nancy's left eyebrow twisted into an "S."

"Aha!" she shouted.

The crowd gasped simultaneously. Nancy's eyes locked in on me like a ballistic missile.

"Val Fremden! *You* didn't vote!"

Oh, crap on a cracker!

With everything else going on, I guess I'd forgotten all about it.

My gut gurgled. The outcome of this year's bake-off was now down to...*me!*

Who should I vote for? Nancy or Laverne?

My mind swirled with panic and confusion. I'd been the one who'd instigated the whole "Let's Make Nancy Kiss a Pig" campaign. I couldn't go against it now. The entire neighborhood was counting on me!

This was our chance to passive-aggressively stick it to the woman who'd made it her civic duty to leave notes on our windshields informing us it was high-time we washed our cars, trimmed our hedges....

"Well?" Nancy said. Her ice-blue eyes cut through me.

Be a patriot, Val. Vote for Nancy's brownies.

I took the clipboard from Doris and wrapped my fingers around the pen chained to it. Everywhere I looked, the expectant, smirking faces of my neighbors stared back.

I smiled back.

Yes, that's right folks. We've got this one in the bag. Pucker up, Nancy, it's time for you to smooch a swine!

The pen in my hand was poised on the paper, ready to tick the box for brownies, when my eyes landed on Laverne. My silly, goofball friend was crouched beside the cage, beaming at the little piglet, her face full of childlike wonder. She was positively moonstruck...or, perhaps, more accurately, "pigstruck."

I felt as morally torn as a Baptist who'd just been handed a free case of Jack Daniels.

"Vote now!" Nancy demanded.

I took a deep breath, closed my eyes and scrawled my vote on the clipboard, then handed it back to Doris. Having sealed my fate, I sidled over to Laverne and slipped my arm around her, to help brace her for the results.

Doris cleared her throat, shot a side look at Nancy, and said, "The winner of this year's bake off is...Laverne and her snickerdoodles!"

"Weeee! I get to kiss the pig!" Laverne squealed with delight and jumped up and down like a little girl.

"Congratulations," I said, and tried to avoid the sour glares of the crowd encircling us.

"I get to kiss a pig!" Laverne squealed again. "Thank you, everybody!"

Laverne gave us all a good gander at her dentures, then toddled over to join the Cub Scout kneeling by his piglet's cage.

"Well, at least *she* looks happy," Tom said.

"Yeah. She does," I said.

We all watched the old Vegas showgirl pucker up.

"Good choice," Jake whispered.

"What do you mean?" I asked. "I just betrayed *everyone*."

"Not *every*one." Jake pointed a hairy finger toward Laverne and the pig. "I see two creatures over there that seem *more* than okay with the outcome."

I had to admit, both the piglet and Laverne appeared ecstatic to have found each other.

"So, you're not mad at me?" I asked.

"No," Jake said. "Why should I be?"

"Because I said I was gonna vote for Nancy."

"On the contrary. You saved us both some bother."

"What do you mean?"

Jake scratched a hairy forearm.

"Val, if you'd a voted for Nancy, I was gonna have to call the ASPCA."

Chapter Fourteen

"Well, there went two days of my life I'll never get back," Tom quipped.

I looked up from my computer. Tom was standing in the doorway of my home office holding a white paper bag. It was a few minutes past seven o'clock, and he'd just returned from picking up Chinese food for dinner.

I snapped my laptop shut. There was no need for him to know I'd been online shopping for slipcovers.

"You can say that again," I said, and eyed the bag in his hand. "Did we clear enough money from the yard sale to get eggrolls?"

"Just barely." Tom looked past me to my desk. "Hey, what's in the envelope?"

My body froze for a microsecond, then thawed enough to fake a casual shrug.

"Nothing."

I glanced at the innocent-looking manila envelope on my desk. Inside it was the lawsuit Finkerman had served me with earlier in the day. It was pure claptrap. A frivolous, long-winded long-shot from a frizzy-haired freak. And it had me worried enough to almost lose my appetite.

I picked up the envelope and shoved it in a drawer.

"Just writer stuff," I lied.

Just like with the slipcover plan, there was no need to get Tom involved. I'd find my own way out of Finkerman's trap. Besides, if I told

Tom, I'd have to confess that I'd traded Laverne's cookies to Finkerman *for a figurine.*

I slammed the drawer shut and smiled up at Tom.

"Did you get the General Tso's chicken like I asked?"

"Of course, your majesty," Tom said. "I want to sleep in the bed tonight...not the doghouse."

I laughed. "Good boy. I see I trained you well."

"I try. Besides, in a few more days, the doghouse will be occupied."

"Oh my gosh! That's right! The puppy comes home in less than a week! And we still haven't come up with a name for it yet."

"How about General Tso?" Tom joked.

I scratched my chin and pretended to consider it. "Nah. Too ethnic."

Tom laughed. I gave him a peck on the lips, turned the light off in my office, and tugged him toward the kitchen.

"Come on, Lieutenant Foreman. I'm so hungry I could eat a horse."

"With everything battered and fried and covered in sweet and sour sauce, Val, who knows? You just might get your wish."

"HAVE YOU SEEN MY FOOTBALL?" Tom asked, then crammed a chopstick full of noodles into his mouth. He shifted his weight in the hideous Barcalounger, set the greasy paper carton in his lap and took a slug of beer.

Suddenly, as if I'd been struck by a blue-white bolt of lightning, my hair stood on end, and my eyes were blinded by a horrific vision of the future.

Tom's shiny blond hair had morphed into a greasy grey ponytail. He had a beer gut big enough to use as a TV tray. And he was sitting in that same, brown-plaid horror of a lounge chair

I nearly choked on my chopsticks.

"You okay?" Tom asked.

"Uh...yeah. I mean, no. No, I haven't see your football."

Not since that guy swapped me a figurine for it at the yard sale.

"Huh. That's weird," Tom said.

"Why?" I asked, and blinked repeatedly until Tom returned to his normal, handsome, well-groomed, present-day self. Unfortunately, the chair remained unchanged.

"I was gonna give it to the puppy," Tom said. "You know, for a toy."

Tom leaned forward in his chair. "Aren't you excited, Val? On Saturday, Sir Albert Snoggles, III is ours!"

My upper lip snarled. "Tell me you didn't just say Snoggles."

"Why? What's wrong with *that* for a name?"

"Uh...*everything*."

Tom frowned. "That's not fair."

"Are you *serious?* What about Rover? Or Rocky? Something...I dunno...*normal*."

"You mean *boring*."

"I mean not *disgusting*, Tom. Snoggles? Gross! I almost lost my appetite."

Tom eyed my plate. "That'd be the day."

I dropped my chopsticks.

"Really, Tom. Snoggles? It sounds like...I dunno. A phlegm-ridden hog rooting around in a slime pit!"

Tom scowled and stabbed at his noodles.

"It was the name of my dog when I was a kid."

The corners of my mouth stretched downward. "Oh. Sorry."

Tom shrugged. "Eh. No big deal. I was eight years old. Back then, disgusting was kind of what I was going for. Maybe you don't know this, Val, but when you're a *boy*, disgusting is *cool*."

"In that case, I'm glad you're not a boy anymore."

Tom grinned coyly. "So, does that mean you don't think I'm disgusting?"

"Tom, there's only one time when I find you truly disgusting."

Tom's face grew serious. "When?"

I smirked. "When you're sitting in *that chair*."

Tom laughed, then waggled his eyebrows at me. "Come sit in my lap, little girl."

I tried not to laugh. "No."

"Come on. I promise not to be *disgusting*."

I bit my lip. "Nothing doing."

Tom picked up the takeout bag on the coffee table. "I'll give you my egg roll if you do."

I eyed him dubiously. "Is it still hot?"

Tom winked a devilish, sea-green eye at me. "*I* like to think so."

"You *do*, huh?"

I grinned and set my take-out box on the coffee table. "Well, let *me* be the judge of that."

I PEEKED OUT FROM UNDER the jumble of bedcovers. Something wasn't right. Something was...*missing*.

I looked up at the ceiling. "Tom, where's Goober's dreamcatcher?"

"Huh?" he grumbled, half asleep.

"Goober's redneck dreamcatcher. Where is it?"

"I put it out in the garage."

"Why?"

Tom rolled over to face me. "I thought that's what you wanted."

"What I wanted? Why would you think that?"

"Well, I found it on the bed a couple of days ago. And correct me if I'm wrong, but wasn't it *you* who kept telling me that you wanted to get rid of all the 'man junk' cluttering up the place?"

I raised up on one elbow. "I'm gonna go get it."

"Uh...you can't."

"Why?"

"It's gone. I...uh...kind of sold it in the yard sale."

I shot up in bed. "You did *what?* How *could* you?"

"What's the big deal, Val? I was there when you carried that thing into the house. Remember? You were so mortified the neighbors would see it that you hid it behind your purse. Come on, Val. Compared to *that* thing, *my chair* looks like a million bucks."

"No it doesn't!" I yelled. "And that was *then*, Tom. Before Goober...you know...*left*. Now I *want* his dreamcatcher."

"For what?"

"For...it has *sentimental* value, okay?"

"Sentimental?" Tom snorted. "I didn't think you knew the meaning of the word."

I raised my bed pillow over Tom's head. "Are you trying to commit assisted suicide?"

"Be honest, Val. You don't hold onto *anything.*"

Pain stabbed my heart like a knife. "*What do you mean by that?*"

Tom sat up beside me in bed. He tried to hug me, but I swatted his arms away.

"Val, when I met you, you owned as close to nothing as a person can get. *Stuff* just doesn't seem to have much meaning to you."

"How do you figure that?"

"Well, like when you got this house. It was full of your parents' junk, and you didn't keep a single scrap of it."

"I did, *too*," I argued. "I kept their *pictures*. And the dragonfly pendant."

I touched the charm hanging around my neck, then tugged it toward Tom as proof. "See?"

Tom tried again to wrap his arms around me. But I just wasn't in the mood for consolation.

"Okay," Tom said. "I get it. I'm sorry about the dreamcatcher. But Val, you should know that's how life goes by now. Some things just disappear, no matter how hard you try to hold onto them."

My heart pinged with pain again.

"I guess…. But *this*…. Oh, Tom. Now I'll *never* see Goober or his dreamcatcher again!"

"Don't be so dramatic. Just call the guy."

"Goober? Don't you think I've *tried*, Tom? His number's been disconnected."

"Not Goober. The guy who bought the dreamcatcher."

"What? How can I do *that?*"

"I saw him give you his card yesterday. You know. That frizzy-headed doofus with the pink sunglasses."

Chapter Fifteen

I woke up on the daybed in my home office with a stabbing pain in my neck. The sun glared through a slit in the blinds, piercing my retinas like a laser beam.

My worst nightmare had come true.

I'd had a giant blowout with Tom last night over Goober's dreamcatcher. But that wasn't it. Neither was the fact that all my neighbors thought I was a scab, thanks to my traitorous bake-sale vote.

Those were mere dust bunnies under the bed of life compared to the bombshell I'd been blasted with last night.

If I was ever going to see Goober's dreamcatcher again, I was going to have to make nice...with Ferrol Finkerman.

My jaw tightened hard enough to crack concrete. If ever in my life I needed a figurine fix, this was it.

I punched the pillow that had given me a sore neck. Good thing my Hammer of Justice was secured safely out of my reach.

I'd made sure of it myself.

Right after my bet with Tom, I'd stuck the hammer inside a tackle box, padlocked it, and then duct-taped it to a rafter in the attic. As much as Tom liked to think *he* knew me, *I* knew myself even better. After all, I was from the South...sort of.

Most folks who grew up on the warm side of the Mason Dixon line had a tendency toward patience, graciousness, and hospitality. My roots dictated that this should be my legacy as well. But as a baby, I'd been transplanted, so my roots never grew that deep.

And let's face it, even a Southern Belle had her limits.

Precautions like the one I'd taken with my hammer were personal fallback strategies that slightly less genteel women such as myself arranged from time to time, in order to retain our dignity when dealing with dirtbags...

...and, of course, to avoid incarceration.

I sat up in the daybed and peeked out between a slit in the blinds. Tom's SUV was gone. I slumped back onto the daybed.

I guess Tom was as ticked as I was. This was the first time he'd left for work without saying goodbye.

The fact that I'd stomped all over the neatly polished work shoes he'd left by the front door had probably done nothing to improve his attitude.

I blew out a breath, dragged myself out of bed, and stumbled over to my desk. I pulled out the manila envelope I'd stuck in the drawer and studied the business card that sleaze-ball Finkerman had stapled to the front of it.

Finkerman & Finkerman, Attorneys at Law
Two Finkermans, No Waiting.
Call 1-888-SUE-EM-NOW.
Good lord! Don't tell me there's two of him!

I set the card back on my desk and peeked through the blinds again. Tom's SUV still wasn't there. I felt the air escape from deep within my lungs.

The fight we'd had last night really wasn't much of one, as domestic quarrels went. Like a total jerk, Tom had refused to argue over what he'd labeled, "a simple misunderstanding." *I* was the one who'd thrown a hissy fit and stomped off to sleep in another room.

A "simple misunderstanding?"
Men!

I blew out an angry breath and padded barefoot to the kitchen. A cappuccino was waiting for me on the counter, along with a note scribbled on the back of an envelope.

I'm sorry, Val. I didn't know that Goober's dreamcatcher meant that much to you.

Tom

I bit my lip until I almost drew blood.

Dang it! Why am I always the one left to feel guilty over something that wasn't even my fault?

I took a sip of cappuccino. It was still warm.

As the foamy brew went down my throat, it began to melt the block of ice in my heart. I took another sip and suddenly, for some reason I couldn't name, I broke down and balled my eyes out like a scolded child.

Chapter Sixteen

Put the ladder back, Val.

P I was in the garage, standing on the bottom rung, directly below the attic access.

Three weeks and six days. You can make it.

The tendons in my jaw tensed as I set my resolve. I stepped off the ladder and dragged it back to its spot against the wall. From the top of the washing machine, a small, grimacing man on a toilet stared back at me.

Doo-Doo Daddy had been liberated from my secret shoebox stash. But I hadn't smashed him...*yet.*

My teeth raked across my bottom lip.

This is gonna to be a lot harder than I thought.

I grabbed Dr. Dingbat's miniature monstrosity and stomped back inside. But on my way to put the figurine back in the closet, something even more grotesque caught my eye. Tom's insidious chair.

I circled the pathetic, plaid-covered lump, studying every detail as if it were in a lineup, suspected of murder. For an easy chair, Tom hadn't been so easy about letting it go.

Why?

Why does Tom want to hold onto this ghastly thing, anyway? What's so important about it? What's his secret? His "sentimental" reason? Was it...memories of another woman?

My fingers tightened around the figurine in my hand. My need for stress relief was approaching nuclear meltdown. But with porcelain pounding temporarily off the table, it was time to initiate Plan B.

Donuts.

I stuck my tongue out at the chair and sneered.

At that moment, I realized I was losing it.

I needed to get out of there before I did something rash. I tossed Difficult Defecation into my purse, grabbed my car keys, and set my sights on Winky's donut shop on Sunset Beach.

I WAS CRUISING DOWN Gulf Boulevard with the top down on Maggie when the flashing lights of a newly installed pedestrian crosswalk made me slam on the brakes. The sudden deceleration sent my purse careening across the passenger seat onto the floorboard.

As I reached down to retrieve it, I realized I was so desperate for one of Winnie's peanut butter and bacon donut bombs that I could already smell it.

It must be my imagination....

I grabbed my purse and sat back up in the seat.

Or maybe it's the two tourists crossing the street in front of me.

The sickly sweet aroma of tropical sunscreen melded with the exhaust from Big Bob's Breakfast Buffet across the street. The combination filled the air and followed along with the couple like a noxious cloud.

I winced. But not just from the smell.

One glance at the hapless pair had me predicting their future...with no need of a crystal ball.

Even in overcast weather like today, the summer sun in Florida was a sneaky devil. From June to September, the lily-white skin of naïve tourists could get par-boiled in under twenty minutes. Judging from the looks of those two, their twenty minutes had come and gone a couple of hours ago.

The doomed duo were a shade of ruddy pink that could only mean one thing. They'd be spending the rest of their vacation lying in bed, covered with aloe-vera gel, blisters, and regrets.

As the couple stepped onto the opposite curb, I hit the gas.

I hope they have enough sense to head for some shade....

Maggie'd barely gotten rolling again when I had to stop a second time. I got caught at the traffic light in front of the Grand Plaza Hotel. It was as if the universe could smell my desperation – even over Bob's odiferous Breakfast Buffet.

I looked over at the round, eleven-story hotel. The Grand Plaza stuck out like a giant alabaster thumb between its neighbors, a pair of dated, blocky, low-rise motels you could drive by a dozen times and never recall.

But you'd have been hard pressed to miss the Grand Plaza. It was brilliant-white, cylindrical, and dotted with rows of dark, square windows. Ever since the first time I saw it, it's reminded me of a toilet-paper tube that'd been branded by a waffle iron.

Built in a bygone era, the place's claim to fame was a rotating restaurant on the top floor. In all the years I'd lived here, I'd never dined there. I guess I just didn't see the point of eating dinner on a merry-go-round. I got seasick just looking off the end of a dock.

The light turned green and I hit the gas. As if on cue, my cellphone rang. The display told me it was Milly. My old friend had a new batch of Pomeranian-mix puppies, one of which would be coming home with me on Saturday.

I'd agreed to take one of the pups off her hands, not so much because I loved dogs as because the whole pregnancy thing was kind of my fault.

A stray dog I'd taken to her dog's Bark-mitzva party a couple of months ago had gotten loose...and a little "rambunctious." Before I could catch him, he'd gone and knocked up Milly's Pomeranian, Charmine.

So, yet again, I was faced with paying the piper for some guy's careless actions.

I answered the phone. "Hey, Milly."

"Hey, Val! You ready to come take this cute little pup of yours off my hands?"

"Sure. We're still on for Saturday pick-up, like we planned."

"Good. I was beginning to wonder. You haven't been by to visit in a while."

"Look, I'm driving, so I can't talk now."

"Val, are you trying to avoid me or something?"

"No." I sighed. "Milly, you know Charmine hates me."

"No she doesn't!"

I waited a beat.

"Okay. She does," Milly confessed. "Sorry about that. So, I'll see you Saturday, then?"

"All right. Bye."

"Oh! Wait!"

"What?"

"By the way, I just want you to know, I think your little Sir Albert Snoggles, III is the pick of the litter!"

My ears started burning.

"*Snoggles?*"

"It's such an adorable name!" Milly cooed. "I hope I spelled it right when I put it on the vaccination records. How'd you and Tom come up with it?"

I unclenched my jaw enough to say, "It was totally Tom's idea."

"Well, he sure is special. I'm gonna miss having all these cutie-pies around. Okay, I'll let you go. See you Saturday for brunch!"

"Okay. See you then."

I clicked off the phone and stomped the gas pedal. Maggie's dual, glass-pack muffler roared so loud it caused a tourist crossing the road to jump clean out of his flip-flops. I waved a lame apology, then hooked a right and headed toward Sunset Beach, where Winky and Winnie's donuts awaited.

If this keeps up, it's gonna be a two-dozen kind of day....

Chapter Seventeen

As I twisted barefoot in the sand toward Winky's little donut shack on Sunset Beach, I couldn't help but notice that he'd made a few improvements to the place.

They weren't nearly enough.

Despite a new coat of light-blue paint, the single-story, concrete-block structure looked more like an abandoned storage unit than a snack shop. The only signs of life around the derelict structure were a couple of seagulls fighting over a wayward French fry – and the unmistakable sound of Winky impersonating Woody the Woodpecker.

The distinct, high-pitched staccato laugh wafted out of the only window on the side of the unkempt building. The panes of the window slid sideways, like a drive-thru service window. But the shack itself was plunked down in pure beach sand, so the only vehicle that could have made it there was an ATV. Or maybe a dune buggy.

Or a customer on foot.

As I made my way through the sand to the walk-up window, I noticed a warped, grey board hanging down from the roof soffit. Rounded at both ends, it resembled a crude, redneck surfboard. Across the middle, hand-painted in yellow, were the words, *Winnie and Winky's Bait & Donut Shop*.

On either side of the words, two smiley faces leered at impending customers. One had hair. One didn't. Both looked a little crazed.

How apropos.

Despite their home-grown efforts to spruce up the place, the donut shop was still a dump, no matter which way you looked at it. But on the beach, neighborhood dives like Winky and Winnie's were treasured for being a tad tarnished. Locals called it "character." Snooty transplants called it "negligence."

To each his own.

Winky's lunatic laugh rang out again, reminding me that I, myself, was *not* in a humorous mood. In fact, just the opposite. Tom had sold Goober's dreamcatcher right out from under me, and I was none too happy about it.

I stuck my head in the service window and spotted Winky.

Dressed in raggedy cargo shorts and a t-shirt with both sleeves ripped off, Winky looked more like a derelict that'd been stranded there overnight than he did the place's rough-shod owner. He was leaning against a worktable, engrossed in a periodical. From the picture on its cover, it was either *Time* or *Mad Magazine*. I never could tell the two apart.

"What's so funny?" I grumbled at the ginger-haired hillbilly.

Winky looked up from his magazine. When he saw me, he half-squelched a snort. The effort looked painful.

"*Pshaw!* Good lordy, Val! You look mad as all get out!"

"Yeah, well, just gimme a donut and a cup of coffee. And keep 'em comin."

Winky's left eyebrow shot up an inch. He saluted and said, "You got it, chief," then disappeared into the inner workings of the shack.

I removed my head from the window and took a calming breath of salt air. My donut fix was on its way.

I glanced toward the beach and noticed that a raw-plywood counter had been tacked to the side of the shop's exterior wall. It appeared to have been suspended with bent nails and at least one entire roll of yellow duct tape. The overall effect looked more like a crime scene than a dining counter.

I dragged a dilapidated barstool up to it and tested the counter's holding power with an elbow. Winky reappeared at the window.

"I see you're expanding the business," I quipped.

"Yep," Winky said.

I reached over and he handed me a cup of coffee.

"Got so's there's so many folks hangin' 'round here the city code feller tole me it was either add seatin' or put up a 'No Loitering' sign. As I'm a big fan a loiterin' myself, I couldn't see doin' that. It'd be like livin' in a state a perpetual irony. You know what I mean?"

"Yeah," I said. *More than you could ever know.*

I grabbed the coffee cup and plopped my purse on the counter. Suddenly, I heard a groan like my grandpa used to make whenever he read the obituary column.

The makeshift plywood countertop listed to the left, broke off the wall, and collapsed onto the sand like a tourist full of tequila shots.

"Lord a-mighty!" Winky bellowed, and craned his head out the window for a look.

Before I could even survey the damage, Winky was at my side, patting my hand.

"You didn't go an' get yourself scalded, now, did ya?" he fussed.

"Huh?" I looked absently at the full coffee cup in my hand. By some miracle, I hadn't even spilled a drop. "No. I'm fine."

"Whew! Sorry about that. Here, lemme help ya pick up your pocketbook stuff."

I set my coffee inside the service window and squatted down beside Winky as he scrabbled around in the sand and weeds, collecting up the contents of my spilled purse.

"Boy howdy!" Winky whistled. "That there's a beaut. Good thing no harm come to this here feller."

"Huh?" I asked, and looked over in his direction.

Perched in Winky's pudgy, freckled paw was the crappy figurine that, a mere fifteen minutes ago, had compelled me onto a ladder in my garage so I could fetch a hammer and smash its little brains out.

"Give that here," I said, and grabbed for the stupid little man on a toilet. Winky swatted my hand away.

"Hold your horses, Val. Lemme have a good look-see at it first."

Winky studied Dr. Dingbat's ode to the throne as if it had been sculpted by Leonardo DaVinci.

"What's this here do?" he asked, and pressed a brown button at the base of the figurine.

I guess all of the figure's other appalling features had caused me to miss that particular one.

Winky mashed the button again.

"Huh. Nothin' happened," he said, and scratched his ginger buzz-cut.

My nose crinkled.

"What's *supposed* to happen?" I asked, then waved my open palm at him wildly. "Wait! I don't want to know!"

But it was too late. Winky's thumbnail had unscrewed a fastener on the base. A lid popped open.

"Looks like the battery's done gone dead," he said, and turned the figurine over and shook it. An old, brown battery dropped into his waiting palm like a dead palmetto bug.

"Too bad. I guess we'll never know," I said with a certain amount of relief.

"Not a problem," Winky said, oblivious to my tone. "I can fix that up right 'cheer. I keep me a mess a batteries around – for all them smoke detectors, don't 'cha know."

Before I could object, Winky trotted inside the shack and returned with a new battery. With the joyful anticipation of a kid at Christmas, he inserted the new battery, closed the lid and mashed the button.

Difficult Defecation grunted like a wild boar at rutting season.

Ugh! How did my life come to this?

Winky laughed like an epileptic chipmunk and mashed the button again. Speechless, I shook my head as he stared with open-faced joy at the statuette and its pornographic sound effects.

"Now *that there's* a pure work a art," he said. "Where'd you get him, Val?"

"At the yard sale."

"Dag nab it!" Winky bellowed. His lips pursed to white. "I wished I'd a gone earlier. But Winnie wouldn't let me. Saturday's our biggest mornin' here at the shop."

Winky eyed the figurine, then me.

"What you gonna do with him, Val? Pardon my askin', but this don't seem like yore kinda thang."

"Uh...I was going to –"

"Val!" Winnie called from the window. "Is that you?"

"Yeah!" I called back.

Winnie's sweet, pudgy face peered out the window. Her black bob hung down either side of her cheeks and she squinted at me through her red-framed glasses. "How are you? You here for one of my famous peanut-butter bombs?"

I jumped at the chance to change of subject. "Does a bear poop in the woods?" I called back.

"He shore does!" Winky answered, and pushed the button on Doo-Doo Daddy again. It grunted like my mother Lucille did every time she tried to rock her big behind out of her easy chair.

"Gimme that!" I said, and snatched the figurine from Winky's hands.

Inside the shack, Winnie grinned and shook her head, sending her black bob swaying around her puffy cheeks. "Winky, I think the grease vat needs changing," she hollered through the window.

"*All right!*" Winky cheered. He puffed out his chest, grinned like a loony toon, and skittered off back inside.

"Change a grease vat?" I asked Winnie after he'd disappeared.

She laughed and shrugged. "Don't ask me why, but it's his favorite thing to do."

As Winnie handed me a donut through the service window, she caught sight of the figurine. "Where'd you get *that* horrible thing?"

"At the yard sale. You didn't hear it?"

"Hear what?"

"The grunting and groaning."

"Oh. Yeah. But I thought it was Winky."

"Nope." I held up the figurine. "It was this little yard sale treasure."

"Yard sales," Winnie said dreamily. She rested her elbows on the service counter and laid her chubby chin in her hands. A faraway look filled her eyes.

"Gosh, Val. You know, if I had all the money in the world, I'd buy me a You-Haul-It and just go yard salin' every single day."

I grinned at the woman who, by some kind of redneck miracle, had been at the perfect place at the perfect time to become the perfect companion for Winky, the most imperfect man I knew.

"Not a bad plan, Winnie," I said. "Hey. By the way, do you happen to know anything about slipcovers?"

Winnie snorted and came up off her elbows. "Come on, Val. You saw the couches Winky picked out for our trailer. What do *you* think?"

I shot her a smile and took a huge bite of Winnie's almost-world-famous peanut butter and bacon donut. One chew into it, my cellphone rang. Of course.

It was Mr. Scam Likely calling again.

"I gotta get this," I mumbled to Winnie through a mouthful of donut. She nodded and disappeared inside the shack.

"You don't waste any time, Finkerman," I said into the phone.

"In keeping with that theme, let's cut to the chase, Fremden," Finkerman's nasal voice whined. "Did you read the summons? I'm suing you for defamation of character."

"Not possible, Finkerman. You don't have any character."

"Ha. Ha. Just for that, I'm doubling my request for damages to five grand."

"Five grand!"

"Yes. See you in court. Unless, of course, you want to settle."

"Argghh!" was the only vocal sound I could manage as a reply. I mashed the red End Call button so hard my cellphone chirped.

"You all right?" Winky asked, his head reappearing in the service window. "You sounded just like that there figurine thangy."

"Yeah, I'm okay," I lied.

Winky studied me as thoughtfully as a man with few thoughts could. "You come up in here mad as a hornet, and now you're bellerin up a storm. What's got in your drawers, Val?"

"Finkerman. He just hit me with a defamation of character suit."

Winky looked at the figurine on the window ledge and smirked. "Don't you mean *defecation* a character?"

I scowled. Finkerman had just pushed my already bad mood over a cliff. Winky's stupid joke was the last straw.

"This isn't *funny*, Winky!" I screeched. "If I don't mount some kind of defense against that parasitic creep, I could be out five grand!"

Winky whistled. "Wow. Five grand. That's a lotta donuts."

"You aren't kidding. That opportunistic dirtbag! If I saw him right now, I'd punch him in the nose!"

"Well, as far as I can tell, that sorry rascal don't need no more bad luck."

"What are you talking about, Winky?"

Winky shrugged. "Nothin', really. I seen him the other day, and, I guess you might say that man was in what my momma would'a called 'a state of dire straits.'"

"Huh? What do you mean?"

"Here. Lemme show ya."

Winky picked up his cell phone, swiped the screen a couple of times, then turned the display to face me. Glaring at me in full color like a miniature TV was a screen shot of Finkerman standing in line at Walmart with a three-pack of Fruit-of-the-Loom tidy whities in his hand. The back of his pants were smeared with, well, you-know-what.

My jaw nearly hit the sand.

"Now *that there's* what I'd call one crappy situation," Winky snorted. "Wouldn't ya say?"

"Yes!" I hollered, and grabbed the phone from Winky's hand so fast he jumped back as if he'd been bitten by a rattlesnake.

"What in blue blazes?" he yelped.

I looked at the photo again, cheered, and reached into the window to give him a huge hug.

"Wallace J. Winchly, I could *kiss* you right now!"

Winky puffed out his chest and stuck his thumbs in the ragged holes where his shirt's sleeves used to be.

"Yeppers," he said, smiling proudly. "I seem to have that effect on women."

I grinned, and from somewhere inside the shack, I heard Winnie burst out laughing.

Chapter Eighteen

Nothing sweetened a sour mood quite like incriminating evidence on a dirtbag.

I took another disbelieving peek at the image Winky sent to my cellphone. It had to have been too good to be true.

But no. There it was. Finkerman in all his waspish glory, in line at Walmart buying undies and looking more than just a little, shall we say...*indisposed.*

"Yes!" I cheered again, and laughed out loud. "This is gonna be just the ticket to put me back on top with that scum bag. Winky, how can I ever thank you?"

"Give me a hand with this here plywood countertop," he said. "I gots to haul it to the dumpster over there."

"You giving up on sit-down service?"

"Naw. But I got me a policy, Val. Duck it or chuck it. I done tried to duck tape that thing to the wall. Now it's time to chuck it."

"What'll you do then about the code guy? You know, the loitering complaints?"

"Don't rightly know," Winky said, and picked up one end of the plywood. "To tell you the truth, Val, the troubles of two honest, hard-workin' country folks don't amount to a hill of pork'n'beans in this here world."

I lifted the other end and helped tote the makeshift counter to the dumpster.

"I've got an idea," I said. "Why don't you get some tables instead?"
Winky dropped his end of the counter.

"Waa hoo! That's a good idea," he said, and stared at me with admiration on his freckled face. "You know, Val, if 'n you ever need a job, the Donut Shop could use a smart gal like you."

"Thanks Winky. I'll keep that offer in my back pocket. As Plan B."

I TOOK A SIP OF COFFEE and waved the flies away from my donut. From my vantage point at the service window, I could see Winnie fiddling around with a wad of dough. Winky was nearby, gleaning business advice from Alfred E. Newman.

As I weighed my options as to what to do next, a small, white ghost crab skittered across my foot and ducked into a hole in the sand.

If only life were that easy.

Finkerman's nasty call had made it crystal clear that my original plan to make nice with him in order to get Goober's dreamcatcher back had been a farcical pipe dream. As far as I could tell, Ferrol Finkerman was completely immune to the subtleties of non-sadistic human behavior.

If I was going to bring down the frizzy-haired shark, I was going to need a sharp spear. The Walmart picture was a good start. But knowing Finkerman, it wouldn't be enough to get him to drop his five-thousand-dollar lawsuit against me.

To achieve that, I was going to have to tip my spear with poison...and aim it precisely where it would do the most damage. Seeing as how Finkerman appeared to lack both a heart and a conscience, I had to figure out the cad's Achilles heel. But what could be worth more to Finkerman than money?

His Hummer? His office? His reputation?

I took another look at the picture of him at Walmart. One thing was for sure. It certainly wasn't his dignity.

If I was going to take Finkerman down, I needed a brilliant, fool-proof plan. Luckily, I was fortified with a belly full of coffee and donuts. And I was already at the place where I'd stumbled upon most of my good ideas in the past.

Sunset Beach.

Of course, Glad was no longer there sprawled in her pink lounge chair, waiting to spout her crazy, but *uncannily sage* advice. Still, I always felt closer to her when I wandered the shoreline by her favorite old haunt, Caddy's beach bar.

I said my goodbyes to Winnie and Winky, then kicked off my sandals and made my way through the sand toward the turquoise water of the Gulf of Mexico.

As my toes dug into the warm sand, I remembered I'd come to the donut shop wearing a bathing suit under my sundress.

I supposed that was irrefutable proof that I truly was a bona fide native of the Sunshine State.

Chapter Nineteen

The hot breeze smelled of salt and seawater as I picked my way along a stretch of sugar-white sand as wide as a football field.

With Winky's donut shop behind me, I still had two buildings to pass as I made my way to the shoreline. As different as night and day, the structures were a tangible reminder that time marches on, and no matter how much we want it to, nothing ever stays the same.

To my left was a familiar refuge, Caddy's beach bar. It was my old stomping grounds, and where I'd first met Winky, Jorge and Goober. The nearly dilapidated old shack was filled with the memories of Florida's laid-back past...of *my* past – including the spirits of Glad and Tony, the long-lost parents I barely knew.

To my right, a hundred feet away from the run-down bar, was its newest neighbor. It was an angular, three-story, orange-colored house that poked out of the dunes like the petrified tooth of a gigantic, prehistoric Jack o' lantern. This intrusive, unfamiliar place belonged to Florida's future...*my* future. Not just because it seemed out of place, but also because it was owned and occupied by a transplant, a new arrival named J.D. Fellows, aka Laverne's boyfriend.

Like Finkerman, J.D. was an attorney. But there, the two men parted ways like chocolate and vanilla.

J.D. had money. Finkerman was perpetually broke. J.D. had a soft side. Finkerman was a hard case. Finkerman was tall. J.D. was short, until you factored in personal integrity – then J.D. soared heads taller than Finkerman.

And when it came to what the two men would stoop to in order to make a buck...well, I *did* mention that they were both attorneys.

As I got closer to the house, I could see that, just as had been the case at Winky's donut shack, there was a new addition to J.D. Fellows' place as well.

But it wasn't duct-taped to a wall.

It was a "No Trespassing" sign. A politically correct version of "Get Lost."

The antithesis of a welcome mat.

Even though I knew J.D., the red-and-white warning sign that stuck out of the sea oats hit me like a slap in the face. Its hard lines tainted the soft beauty of the quaint, sandy footpath that had been worn into the vegetation over the years by fellow beachgoers.

No stranger to feeling left behind by the upper crust, I reached inside my purse and toyed with the idea of leaving Dr. Dingbat's Difficult Defecation on J.D.'s back porch, as a kind of joke. J.D. was notoriously fastidious, and I was positive the he'd have been horrified by Doo-Doo Daddy. But the diminutive attorney was also a bit paranoid. Knowing him, he would've probably called a bomb squad to have it removed.

I decided against it and let loose of my grip on the figurine. To be honest, it wasn't because I was too *nice* to pull the prank on J.D. Ultimately, I was too *selfish*. After getting another gander at the nasty little thing, I decided I didn't want to miss out on the delicious satisfaction of smashing that little piece of crap to smithereens.

I'D WADED, ANKLE-DEEP, almost half a mile north along the beach to the yellow-and-gold, bumblebee-striped BilMar Hotel. My hands were full of freckled cockle shells and cute, little cat paw shells I'd picked up in the gentle surf along the way.

My skin was sizzling in the midday sun, and I was dying for a dip in the ocean to cool off. I waded to shore, deposited my shells and sandals on the sand, and set my purse on top of my shoes. Then I peeled my sweaty sundress off over my head, dropped it on top of my purse, and waded into the Gulf.

It was as warm as bathwater.

July in St. Pete Beach meant warm seas, hot sun, and plenty of stingrays. The greyish-brown, shovel-shaped creatures congregated in small schools this time of year. Ranging from saucer-sized to as big as cookie sheets, the gentle creatures burrowed into the sand, and were usually nothing to worry about.

Unless you stepped on one.

I'd had the misfortune to do just that a few years back. The top of my foot had been speared by one of their poison-tipped tails.

Just like my run-ins with Finkerman, the stingray's poison had taken weeks to get over, and, in the end, had added absolutely *no* value to *my* life whatsoever, or anyone else's, for that matter. And, just like Finkerman, it was an experience I didn't care to repeat.

Stepping into the water, I shuffled my feet along the hard, sandy bottom. That way, any stingrays lurking nearby would have advanced warning I was headed their way. Once the water was waist high, I lifted my feet and floated, lightly treading water to stay upright.

The salty Gulf water buoyed my body, and I bobbed around in the gentle surf like a roasting cork. I kept an eye on my purse on shore, and wished I'd brought a sunhat. Otherwise, the blue sky and tropical beach created a scene as idyllic as any tourist brochure could conjure. Still, all I could think about was the current mess I was in.

What is it with guys like Finkerman?

What is it with guys in general?

And Tom! How could he have been such a clod? Selling Goober's dreamcatcher – and to Finkerman, of all people!

The man I cared about most had somehow managed to find the man I cared about least, and sold him the only thing I had to remind me of the man I cared about like a brother.

Some dreamcatcher that had turned out to be. More like a nightmare-catcher if you asked me....

But what else should I have expected? If it weren't for the orchestra of ironic twists in my life, I'd never go dancing at all.

Topping the whole disaster off was another ironic doozy; I was living with a cop, but I couldn't ask him to help me find my missing friend.

It was too dangerous. For Tom.

What if it turned out Goober was a felon on the run or something? And that check stub of his for ten grand. It could have been a hit-man payoff, for all I knew.

No. It was too risky to get Tom involved. He could get in deep trouble for aiding and abetting a fugitive...or something like that.

Besides, I'm so mad at Tom right now I could fry his butt in a skillet with a side of bacon....

A seagull screeched overhead, as if heckling my screwed-up life. I splashed water at it and headed for shore. As I did, I thought I heard Glad's toady voice whisper:

"What are you winning, kiddo?"

"Huh?"

"What are you winning, holding onto your anger?"

"I don't know!" I hissed at the seagull.

But I have a feeling I'm about to find out.

Chapter Twenty

On the way home from the beach, I stopped by the bank and picked up three rolls of quarters. I tucked them away inside my purse and set my expression to grim. With my foul mood restored and my hillbilly hacky-sack freshly restocked, I was ready to do battle.

Tom wouldn't even know what hit him.

But alas, my vengeful rampage wasn't to be. When my blond nemesis came home from work, the jerk foiled my plans – in a way I never saw coming.

"YOU FORGIVE ME YET?" Tom asked through a narrow slit in the front door. Like a cop on a routine bust, he'd rung the door bell, then cracked the front door slightly ajar and hollered through the opening while maintaining a safe distance.

"Absolutely not," I said, and grabbed my weaponized purse from the kitchen counter.

Tom poked a bunch of flowers through the crack in the door and waved them around like a white flag of surrender. They were daisies. My favorite.

"Humph!" I responded sourly.

Tom poked his head inside and shot me one of his impossible-to-hate, boyish grins.

"I've got something else for you, too," he said, and slipped a shoulder through the door.

"Forget it," I grumbled. "I am *sooo* not in the mood."

Tom eyed my purse warily, then laughed. "It's a *book*, Val."

I gripped my purse strap tighter. "I'm not in the mood to *read*, either, in case you haven't noticed."

Tom stepped a leg inside, and cautiously extended his arm toward me, as if he were afraid he might lose a limb.

In his outstretched hand was a small paperback entitled, *Precious Names for Precious Pets.* The cover featured a puppy so cute I wanted to claw my eyes out. My jaw unclenched a tiny smidgen.

"What do we need *that* for?" I muttered. "I thought you and Milly already decided on a name *without* me."

Tom stepped the rest of the way inside. "What gave you *that* idea?"

"Milly told me. She put it on the puppy's registration papers."

"Oh. I didn't know. When I talked to her, I just meant it as a placeholder, Val. A joke."

I shot Tom a dirty look. "Ha ha."

"Come on, Val. I got this book so we can decide on a name for the puppy *together.*"

Before I could raise my purse high enough to bop him, Tom stepped up, wrapped his arms around me, and pulled me close. Then he surprised me by shuffling backward like a crab. I wriggled against Tom's chest as he dragged me and my foul mood along with him, like some "emotional repo" man.

"What are you doing?" I asked.

Then I realized what was happening.

I tried to squirm free of his hug, but it was too late. Tom tumbled, butt-first, into his disgusting Barcalounger, pulling me along onto his lap.

As I fell, I lost my grip on my hillbilly hacky-sack. It dropped onto the floor, and let out a groan the likes of which I'd only ever heard emanate from my Uncle Popeye after Thanksgiving dinner.

Oh, good lord! The figurine! It's still in my purse!

I took the only evasive action I could think of. I kissed Tom hard on the mouth, hoping to distract him from the gut-wrenching moan.

"That's a new one," he said, pulling away from my lip-lock.

"What?" I asked, and tried to kiss him again.

"No really. Was that *you*, Val? I mean, are you okay?"

"Uh. Yeah. I ate lunch at Laverne's," I lied.

"Oh," Tom said, and eyed me dubiously. "Well, I was gonna take you out for dinner to make up for, you know, Goober's dreamcatcher."

"Oh." A tinge of relief offered itself up like a booby prize. At least Tom hadn't figured out I was harboring a fugitive figurine in my purse.

"But I guess we'd better order in," he said. "You know, just in case."

"Sure," I said sweetly. "Whatever you say."

"What?" Tom asked.

He craned his head back to get a better look at me. "I never thought I'd hear you say *those words*, Val. Have you got a fever or something?"

Yeah. A fever that nothing short of pummeling porcelain to pieces is gonna cure.

Chapter Twenty-One

I was swimming in the crystal blue Gulf off of Sunset Beach. I took a bite of peanut-butter donut and petted the stingray I was riding on.

All of a sudden, a gigantic grey shadow the size of an elephant swam underneath us, casting a menacing, dark shadow on the sandy bottom. I frantically nudged the sides of the stingray, trying to get it to gallop away to safety.

But it was too late.

The gigantic beast rocketed past us, then circled back around. It blasted a giant breath out of its blowhole, then plowed through the water toward me and the stingray like a renegade torpedo.

Just before it rammed us into oblivion, the behemoth sea monster stopped dead in front of us, causing a wall of breakwater to swoosh over my head. I grabbed onto the stingray's gills for dear life, and nearly tumbled backward, head over heels, from the blast of the powerful wave.

As the wall of water passed, I swiped frantically at my eyes. I was desperate to get a bead on my enemy and what he was up to. The saltwater stung as I blinked in disbelief.

Jutting out of the water right before me was the hideous head of a beastly whale-shark thing. Its long, pointy nose was like that of a sawfish. The top of its head was covered in hairy tentacles that reminded me of a rusty, fraying Brillo Pad.

The creature opened its huge, hideous jaws full of dagger-like, blood-encrusted teeth and said:

"You ready for a cappuccino?"

I cracked an eye open, then pulled the soggy corner of a pillow from my mouth.

"Good morning, princess," Tom quipped.

"Nyeahgh," I said, and raised up on an elbow.

"How about I just set this on the nightstand? Sorry, but I gotta go get dressed. I'm running late."

"Okay, thanks," I muttered.

Tom kissed me on the nose, set the cup down, and turned to leave.

"Hey, Tom?" I called after him.

He turned back to face me. "Yeah?"

"I was just wondering. How many hairs do you need to do a DNA analysis?"

Tom's eyes narrowed. "What?"

"You heard me," I said, and reached for the cappuccino.

"Just one, if it's got a follicle. Why?"

"Just need it for this story I'm working on."

Relief melted the worried edges of his face. "Oh. Okay. Hey, mind if I take some quarters? I've gotta park downtown later today."

"No problem. I've got plenty in my purse."

Tom grinned slyly. "Thought so. Look, no need for you to get up. Take it easy."

"Okay. Thanks."

I watched Tom disappear down the hallway. I took a sip of cappuccino and sighed. Then the caffeine kicked my brain awake and I nearly spewed hot coffee all over the sheets.

Crap on a cracker! My purse! Doo-Doo Daddy's still in there! If Tom sets off another round of grunts from that figurine, I'll be had! Plus, dang it! I forgot! I'm supposed to be mad at him!

"Stay out of my purse!" I screeched and scrambled out of bed like a two-timing hussy.

I slammed the cappuccino on the nightstand, collided with the doorframe, and bounced off the walls down the hall until I spilled out into the living room and nearly rammed right into Tom.

He was leaning across his eyesore of a chair, his butt toward me. He had one hand on the armrest of the Barcalounger, supporting his torso. The other arm was reaching down toward the floor. His fingertips were mere inches away from my purse....

"Don't touch that!" I bellowed.

Tom jumped as if he'd been poked by a hot cattle prod. His right hand instinctively reached for his pistol, but his undies weren't packing. He whirled around to face me.

"What in the world is up with you, Val?"

"Nothing!"

I backpedaled against the adrenaline pumping through my veins.

"It's just that...you know...a woman's purse is her, like, you know...*her sanctuary*, Tom!"

Tom didn't say a word. Instead, he stared at me with an expression he must have honed over three decades of having to listen to idiotic alibis.

"Sanctuary?" he said finally.

"Look, Tom. You go get dressed. I'll get the quarters. How many do you need?"

"Enough for three hours ought to cover it."

"Okay, a whole roll then." I shooed him down the hallway. "Go. Get dressed! I'll take care of it."

As Tom disappeared into the bathroom, my knees nearly buckled with relief.

Geeze. That was a close one.

Twice already I'd had to lie to cover my tracks for carrying around that stupid figurine!

I jerked opened my purse. As I fished for Tom's quarters, a sweaty little guy stared back at me from his perch on a toilet.

From the looks of it, it was pretty clear that *one* of us had some pretty screwed up priorities...and I had a sneaking suspicion it *wasn't* Doo-Doo Daddy.

Chapter Twenty-Two

With Tom and his prying eyes safely away at work, it was time to get serious about my current life situation. Too many things were spiraling out of control. My addled brain was overwhelmed.

I padded over to my desk, grabbed a notebook and jotted down a quick list of my most pressing disasters currently plaguing me.

There were five.

Six, if I counted my figurine addiction.

Geeze! I'm dealing with more catastrophes than the Red Cross!

I glanced over my list.

Current disaster one: Finkerman had Goober's dreamcatcher. On the plus side, I had his unflattering Walmart cameo. I figured this disaster could be resolved with an even swap. Easy-peasy. But then again, nothing involving Finkerman was *ever* easy.

Current disaster two: Finkerman's lawsuit against me. On the plus side...there was no plus side. I had nothing on the jerk big enough to hold back *that* impending fiasco. So far, the poison-tipped spear I needed to slay him still eluded me....

Current disaster three: Tom Foreman's lousy performance as a boyfriend. He'd named the puppy without me and given away a semi-priceless family heirloom. On the plus side, his actions, while thoughtless, weren't intentional. And he had a cute rear end. He'd kind of cleared himself of the puppy-naming wrong-doing last night. But he was still guilty as sin for selling Goober's dreamcatcher to Finkerman.

Not to mention the fact that I still owed him one for that stupid "vibrator in the yard-sale box" prank.

I glanced at a picture of Tom on my desk and smiled like the Wicked Witch of the West.

Oh, no, Tommie dearest. Don't think I've forgotten about that *one!*

Current disaster four: the upcoming week's assignment for *Mystery Writing for Fun and Profit*. On the plus side, I was kind of the teacher's pet. Still, Langsbury's charitable streak was as thin as her papery skin. Thursday night, she'd instructed each of us to do a mock crime scene investigation and report back to her about it this week. So far, I hadn't done squat on the assignment. But it was only Tuesday. I still had two more days to figure that one out.

Current disaster five. Goober was still missing in action. On the plus side....

I chewed my pen. As much as I grumbled about Goober, I couldn't think of a single good thing about him being gone. In fact, the mere thought of my goofy, wooly-mustachioed friend being lost and alone somewhere caused my gut to flop.

I knew that under *normal* circumstances, Goober would be perfectly capable of taking care of himself. But what he'd done – up and leaving like he did – wasn't normal. Something was wrong. Otherwise, why would he have disappeared like that? Why couldn't he tell me or *somebody* what was going on? I mean, what if someone was *after* him or something?

I glanced up at the postcard he'd sent.

If you need me, you know how to catch me.

The word "catch" could've just been a bad pun. But I didn't think so. Even though I'd so far been unable to find one, my gut told me that Goober's dreamcatcher held a clue to how to reach him. Now it was gone. Finkerman had it. And I had to get it back no matter what it took.

I bit my lip and slapped the notebook down on my desk. I hadn't wanted to smash a figurine so bad since...*yesterday*.

I reached for my purse and the toilet-sitting figurine that still lurked inside it. As I did, my phone rang, saving me from losing my bet with Tom for at least another minute or two.

"Hello?"

"Val! It's me, Cold Cuts!"

"Cold Cuts! Hey, stranger! How are things with you and Bill?"

"Good, thanks. Listen, I was wondering. Have you'd heard anything from Goober?"

My body slumped along with my voice. "Not a word. Have you?"

"I got a letter in the mail from him today."

I sprung off my chair. "Really? What did he say?"

"Well, that's just it. He didn't say anything. He just sent a check for $1,200. That's the price we discussed for your...uh...the RV."

"No note or anything?"

"No. Like I said, not a word."

"What about the check? Did it have an address on it?"

"No. It was a cashier's check."

"Dang it! Geeze. I hope he's all right."

"Me, too. Well, look, Val. Some customers just walked in. Let's catch up on Friday, okay?"

"Friday?"

"At Winnie's engagement party."

"Oh my lord! I'd forgotten all about it!"

"Got any idea what to get her?" Cold Cuts asked.

"No. Wait. Winnie mentioned yesterday that she likes going to yard sales. Does that help?"

"Huh. Not really. But...oops. Look, I gotta go. Bye!"

Cold Cuts clicked off the phone. I pictured the cute, bohemian, thirty-something girl with wild brown hair. She must have been standing at the reception desk when she called. I visualized the kitschy,

1950s-Hawaiian style lobby of the Sunset Sail-Away Resort. Bill, her tall, thin, yoga-guru lover was probably right by her side. They made a good team.

I sighed and plucked Goober's postcard from the cork board above my desk and studied it for the millionth time.

Like the cashier's check he'd sent to Cold Cuts, Goober's postcard didn't offer up any new clues. But on the plus side, thanks to Cold Cuts' call, I now knew that my wayward, traveling hobo friend was still alive and kicking.

I TOOK A SLUG OF BEER to deaden the pain and dialed Finkerman's number.

A robotic voice spouted a canned-sounding spiel.

"Thank you for calling the award-winning law offices of Ferrol Finkerman, attorney at law. He's not available right now to –"

"Gimme a break!" I said sourly.

"Excuse me?" the voice said.

"Uh...sorry!" I gasped and nearly fell out of my chair. "I just...uh...somebody here...I just sneezed. Yeah. *Sneezed!* Who is this?"

"I'm Fargo Finkerman, ma'am. Ferrol Finkerman's nephew."

"Oh. Well, uh...could you please tell him I'd like to make an appointment at his earliest convenience?"

"Certainly, ma'am. He should be back from the 7-11 in a couple of minutes...would that work?"

"Uh...not really. How does his schedule look for tomorrow?"

"He's got court until after lunch."

"Okay."

"So, should I schedule you for 1:30?"

"Sure. That would be perfect."

"Who should I say called?"

"Uh...Freda Feldman."

"Will he know you, ma'am?"

"No. I'm a new client."

"And who referred you?"

My mind went blank. I blurted out the first thing to cross my mind. "Umm...the ASPCA."

I clicked off the phone. My heart raced with exhilaration at the incredible, ingenious plan that I, Valiant Stranger, had just hatched on the fly.

I'll just sneak over to Finkerman's office tomorrow morning while he's in court, and steal back Goober's dreamcatcher!

If successful, the plan would solve one problem I had with Finkerman. As for the lawsuit, well, I'd just have to cross that bridge when I came to it.

I WAS HAVING A DATE with Destiny when Tom got home from work early and caught me in the act.

"Val? Are you home?" he called as he walked into the house.

"Uh...yeah."

Crap on a cracked-up cracker!

I was standing in front of the bedroom mirror, squeezed into a disguise I'd worn a couple of years ago during my brief stint working with Cold Cuts and Milly as a spy for Date Busters. I'd put the ridiculous ensemble together myself, and named it "Destiny."

Destiny was a cross between a go-go dancer and a tramp. The outfit consisted of silver stretch hot-pants, a red halter top, KISS-era platform boots and a cheap blonde wig voluminous enough to make Dolly Parton chew her nails off with envy.

I'd planned on wearing the get-up as a disguise when I went to Finkerman's office tomorrow morning. But now Tom had come home early, and I was in a tight spot.

And I didn't mean the hot pants.

The last thing I needed was to be forced to divulge my scheme to Tom. I turned around. The hot cop was standing at the bedroom door, eyeing me with suspicious, sea-green eyes.

Crap! Think of something, Val. Fast!

I smiled and waved casually. "Hey."

Tom did his best to keep a straight face.

"What are you doing?" he asked, and began un-holstering his gun.

"Uh...well, you know...what they...uh...say," I stammered, and nearly lost my balance on the eight-inch platform heels.

Tom stifled a smirk. "No. What do they say, Val?" He looked me up and down, shaking his head.

"You know. That *variety* is the spice of life."

Tom's face went slack. The left corner of his mouth twitched.

I snapped the garter belt around my thigh and quipped, "And you thought I couldn't stay up past 9:30."

"That was a joke," he said, looking as unsure about where this conversation was going as I was.

Geeze, Val. You've really painted yourself into a corner this time. Tom thinks you're a hooker! Or...wait a second...a playful girlfriend with a naughty imagination...?

I bit my lip seductively, tilted my head to one side, and laid on a Southern accent thick enough to stick to the wall.

"Have I ever told you how much I love a guy in uniform, mister cop man? How would you like to –"

Tom's lips never let mine finish that sentence. In under fifteen seconds, we were way past the point of no return. Then I remembered I was supposed to be mad at him.

I forgot. Again!

Geeze. I was definitely slipping in my old age.

Chapter Twenty-Three

Wednesday morning, Tom went off to work and I went off to get ready for my second date with Destiny.

I found her piled in a chair in the corner of the bedroom. The memory of how she'd ended up there made me smile. In that regard, Tom certainly made it difficult to stay angry at him.

I wriggled my butt into the silver hot-pants and stuffed my feet into the platform boots. I slipped the red halter top over my head and tied it at the neck.

The humongous blonde wig was as large and fluffy as a full-grown Pekinese, and almost the same shape, thanks to last night's shenanigans. I planted it on my head and adjusted it in the bathroom mirror.

For makeup, I circled my eyes with eyeliner and coated my eyelids with plum-purple eyeshadow all the way to my eyebrows. For good luck, I plastered on a shade of lipstick red enough to do Glad proud. Then, for a final flourish, I used eyeliner to paint a suspicious mole over the left side of my upper lip.

Voila!

I was no longer Val Fremden...or even Valiant Stranger. I was *Destiny* – undercover private eye and go-go dancer extraordinaire!

And, best of all, totally unrecognizable.

I grinned at my reflection, grabbed my purse, and headed for the door.

AFTER CHECKING THROUGH the front blinds with binoculars to make sure Nancy Kravitz Junior wasn't checking though *her* front blinds with binoculars, I poked my head out the front door and glanced around.

It appeared the coast was clear.

I snuck out, locked the door behind me, and hobbled down the driveway toward Maggie, as fast as my fifteen-pound boots would allow.

I had my fingers on Maggie's door handle when I heard someone call my name.

"Val!"

Oh, crap!

I turned around. Laverne was on her knees in her yard, fiddling around with her garden gnomes.

Great. How am I going to explain this?

"Honey, are you going to the grocery store?" the old Vegas showgirl asked, not even batting an eyelash.

"Uh...sure, Laverne. That's where I'm going all right."

"While you're there, could you pick me up a bottle of kosher water?"

"Kosher wha? Okay. Yeah. Sure."

"Thanks, sugar! I got some money right here." Laverne stuck a hand inside of her hot-pink, skin-tight tube top.

"Uh. That's not necessary," I said.

"Then I'll pay you when you get back, darlin'."

"Okay." I turned, opened the door and slid my sparkling hot-pants across Maggie's bucket seat. I turned the ignition and peeled down the driveway.

"Have a nice day!" Laverne called out, and waved merrily at me as I drove away.

So much for stealth.

She didn't mean to, but Laverne had just totally harshed my Destiny bad-girl buzz.

JUST LIKE FINKERMAN, his office was on the sleazy side of town. With Sultry Sam's Sex Shoppe next door, a hooker in a run-down car blended right into the scenery.

Lucky me.

Graphic ads pasted on Sam's windows reminded me of something on my "To-Do List." Maybe after I'd heisted Goober's dreamcatcher from Fargo Finkerman, I'd pop into the Sex Shoppe and get a "personal item" to pay Tom back for his prank.

I climbed out of Maggie and wobbled like disco Frankenstein toward Finkerman's door. I was reaching for the knob when my phone rang. I checked the screen. It was Winky.

"Hey. What do you want?" I asked.

"Are you sittin' down, Val?" Winky asked, his voice trembling.

"What? No. What's happened?"

I hobbled over and leaned against the dirty wall outside Finkerman's office.

"Well, since you went and got me that Dale Earnhardt Big Gulp cup a couple a weeks ago, I started broadening my horizons."

"Winky, what are you talking about?"

"That dang Dr. Dingbat action figure you showed me, Val. It's worth twenty big ones!"

"Twenty dollars?" I said into the phone.

A guy walking by in a cheap suit stopped in his tracks and eyed me up and down.

"Naw," Winky said. "Twenty *grand*, Val!"

"How much?" I gasped.

"Twenty thousand U.S. greenbacks!"

"I'll give you twenty-five," said the sleazebag in the cheap suit.

I shot him some side eye. "You've got to be kidding me!" I yelled. "Get outta here!"

"I ain't kiddin' Val!" Winky said.

The guy shuffled off toward the sex shop. I turned back to Winky on the phone.

"How do you know that?" I asked.

"That's what I'm trying to tell you, Val. I been lookin' 'round on the Internet. I seen a post on Craigslist. Somebody's offerin' twenty grand for an original Dr. Dingbat Difficult Defecation figurine!"

"Holy smokes!"

"I don't know if he does or not, Val. But you want this gal's number? I done writ it down."

"Yes! Of course! Give it to me."

"I'd like to give it to you," a voice said beside me. Sleazeball was back.

"I told you to get lost!" I hissed.

"So, you don't want her number?" Winky asked.

"What?" I said into the phone, and sneered at cheap suit guy.

"Make up your mind, Val."

"Okay. Yes, Winky. I want the number. What is it?"

I wrote down the lady's name and number on a scrap of paper, and shoved it into my purse. I felt around in my bag for the figurine. Panic shot through me for a second when I couldn't find it. Relief made me sigh when my fingers finally wrapped around it.

I let go of the figure and checked the time on my cellphone. It was 11:37 a.m.

"Look, Winky. Thanks for the info, but I gotta go. My window of opportunity is closing fast."

"You gettin' you a service window, too?" he asked.

"Huh? Oh. Yeah. Something like that. Bye."

I clicked off the phone, yanked the hem a bit lower on my back of my hot-pants, and headed for Finkerman's door.

"LOOK, MR. FINKERMAN said you girls need to make appointments first. No more drop-ins."

I stared, open-mouthed, at the youngster behind the desk. Poor Fargo Finkerman couldn't have been more than twenty. He was a younger, slimmer, slightly less frizzy-haired version of Ferrol Finkerman. Hopefully the poor sap hadn't inherited his uncle's charm and wit to go along with his looks.

I mean, *no one* should be that unlucky.

"An appointment?" I asked, stalling as I sized Fargo Finkerman up. *He thinks I'm a call girl, so I'll give him call girl!*

I struck a provocative pose and nearly fell over head first onto his desk. I steadied myself on my platform boots and shot young Fargo a smile he apparently didn't feel the need to return.

"Yes, an appointment," Fargo said. "We can't have you turning up at all hours. It's bad for business."

"I uh...understand," I said. "It's just that, well, sweetie, I left something behind at my last...uh...*appointment* with Mr. Finkerman, if you know what I mean."

Fargo let out a huge sigh. I'd seen less doomed-looking faces on movie posters featuring the Apocalypse.

"What did you forget?" he muttered, and stared at his desk blotter.

"Well, it was...a thing...with a pair of pink thong underwear strung up on –"

Fargo closed his eyes and put a hand up. "Say no more. *Please.* I'll go get the box."

Finkerman's clone left the room. A moment later, he returned with a cardboard box full of panties and a jumble of assorted plastic gadgets the likes of which I'd never seen before, and hoped to never see again.

"Be my guest," Fargo said in a voice devoid of any hope for the future.

I peered inside the box and got the willies. "Listen, kid. You wouldn't happen to have a pair of rubber gloves on you, would you?"

Fargo closed his eyes for a moment. "In my uncle's office," he sighed.

Fargo didn't invite me to follow him, but I did anyway.

When he cracked open the door to Finkerman's office, I barged in and poked around. While I rifled through the shelves and drawers, Fargo, like a zombie slave, slowly and methodically pulled a pair of latex gloves from a conveniently located, industrial-size box on his uncle's desk.

Drats! Goober's dreamcatcher isn't here!

Fargo handed me the gloves. I followed him back out to his desk at reception. I tugged on the gloves and scrounged through the box, trying not to gag.

"Sorry for the bother, young man," I said as I gave up and pulled off the rubber gloves. "Tell Ferrol that Lady Destiny dropped by."

"Lady Destiny?" Fargo spat, and rolled his eyes. "Gimme a break."

"What do you mean?" I asked, suddenly worried he was on to my plan.

Fargo stared me down with beady eyes slanted with disdain. The family resemblance was so uncanny I nearly winced in sympathy.

"You never had an 'appointment' with my uncle, did you?"

I bit my red-lipstick-smeared bottom lip and cringed.

"Why would you say that?" I asked.

Fargo pursed his lips into a sour scowl.

"Because. You're not his type."

"Really?" I asked, suddenly feeling weirdly inadequate. "So, what's his type?"

Fargo sighed.

"Incoherent, lady. Incoherent."

Chapter Twenty-Four

C *rap on a cracker.*

Raiding Finkerman's office had been a bust. The jerk must've taken Goober's dreamcatcher home with him. Either that, or he had it hanging on the rearview mirror of his obnoxious yellow Hummer.

So much for Plan A.

I stumbled out of Finkerman's office and flopped my scantily-clad fanny down onto Maggie's driver's seat.

I shot back out of the seat as if it had detonated.

"Yeeowwch!"

The July heat had turned Maggie's red vinyl seats into red-hot sheets of semi-molten plastic. My silver hot-pants didn't offer nearly enough protection. What I needed was a pair of butt-potholders.

Strike that.

What I needed was a spare heat shield from a NASA space shuttle.

I rubbed my red thighs and looked around. Thankfully, cheap-suited scuzz-man was nowhere in sight. He'd probably disappeared back inside Sultry' Sam's Sex Shoppe. I didn't care to see him again, so I scrapped the idea of going inside to find something to prank Tom with, and focused on my next urgent mission.

Procuring twenty grand for Doo-Doo Daddy.

I shifted my gaze to the scrap of paper in my hand. On it I'd written the name of the Craigslist nutcase Winky said was willing to pay a fortune for a ceramic replica of a half-naked fat guy grunting on a tiny toilet.

I shook my head.

What's the world coming to?

I set my jaw to "whatever" and punched in the number on my cell phone.

"Yello?" a deep, raspy voice said.

"Hello, is this Layla Lark?"

"Yes. Who's calling?"

"Uh...Val Fremden. I got your number off Craigslist?"

"Oh! Do you have the figurine?!"

"Uh. Yes."

"I *must* have it! When can you bring it to me? Can you do it *now?*"

I looked down at my roasted thighs, sparkly hot pants and shiny vinyl knee boots.

"Uh...I'm kind of indisposed at the moment."

Unless I want to take up the world's oldest profession.

"It's really urgent," the woman said earnestly. "You see, I lost the figurine in a poker game. It belongs to my husband. If I don't get it back by tonight...well...I'm toast!"

"Oh. Well, in that case...uh...do you have the money on you?"

A wolf-whistle sounded nearby. Sleazeball was back, loitering around the door of the sex shop. He shot me a look that should have come in a plain brown wrapper. I turned my back to him.

"Yes. In twenties and fifties," the woman said. "I had a bit of luck at the table Monday night...."

"Okay, then. So, where should we meet?"

"Do you know Davie's Donuts?"

Davie's Donuts? Really? "Yeah."

"Meet you there in say, ten minutes?"

I looked around the sleazy strip mall. Scuzz-ball took a step in my direction. The hair on the back of my neck stood up.

"Hello? Are you still there?" Layla asked.

"Wha...yes. Yes, I'm here."

"So, do you know where Davie's is?"

"Yeah. I do. See you there in ten."

I clicked off the phone. Cheap-suit man was only a few yards away, lumbering toward me like a down-on-his luck insurance salesman. He appeared desperate to sell me something from his portfolio of short-term products....

I jumped back into the fiery fanny fryer and turned the ignition key. My thighs smoked and Maggie's tires squealed as I shifted into reverse and hooked a sharp right. I spun the wheel and shifted into drive. The sleazy guy yelled something at me, but I couldn't hear what he said over the roar of Maggie's dual glasspack muffler.

Finally, I'd caught a break today.

Chapter Twenty-Five

T*wenty thousand bucks!*

As I tooled down Gulf Boulevard, the figure swirled around in my mind like the bubbles in a gin and tonic.

That would be enough to pay off Finkerman, buy a new Barcalounger for Tom, plenty of toys for the new puppy coming Saturday, and even some fancy, insulated seat covers for Maggie! Anything left over, I'd donate to a good cause – namely a huge freezer full of Ben & Jerry's Cherry Garcia....

I angled Maggie left into the parking lot of Davie's Donuts. The lot was empty except for a dark-blue, late-model Cadillac with the vanity license plate, Glam-Bit. I pulled up along the right side of it.

As I opened my door to get out, the tinted, passenger-side window on the Caddy zipped down with a mechanical hum.

A deep voice from within the car's dark interior said, "Get in."

I climbed out of Maggie, tightened my grip on my hillbilly hacky-sack, and peered in the open window. Sitting alone on the driver's side of the Cadillac's huge bench seat was a small-framed, big-bosomed woman somewhere between the ages of sixty and three hundred and fifty years old.

"Layla Lark?" I asked.

"The same. Get in outta the heat, kid."

I opened the door and slid inside. The air conditioning was welcoming. The cigarette smoke, not so much.

Layla swiped an errant hair away from her forehead and crushed out a Virginia Slims Menthol on the carcasses of its fallen comrades, who tumbled from the overflowing ashtray like a spilled platter of albino French fries.

The leather-skinned woman of indeterminate age patted the stiff, grey-brown bun on top of her head with both hands, then spoke with a voice I could only describe as, "the revenge of Virginia Slims."

"Lemme see it," she croaked, and held out a boney hand so laden down with rings and bracelets I was impressed she could even lift it.

"Uh...sure."

I fished around and pulled Dr. Dingbat's Difficult Defecation from my purse.

She snatched it from my hand and mashed the brown button on its base.

Doo-Doo Daddy moaned like a camel giving birth to an elephant.

"Awe, bumfuzzle," the old lady said. "Don't tell me you've gone and changed the battery!"

"Well, yes. So it would work. I don't see –"

"The deal is off," Lark said, and tossed the figurine on the seat between us. She leaned over the steering wheel, rubbed her forehead with her hands, and began muttering unintelligible words that sounded vaguely like the obscenities hurled by cartoon characters.

"What do you mean, *off?*" I asked, incredulous.

"It wasn't the *figurine* I needed," she said. "It was the *battery* inside it."

"Huh?" I said, shaking my head in disbelief. "I don't understand."

The old lady shrugged and looked over at me.

"It's like most collectibles, kid. Once they're out of the original packaging, their worth is exactly horse hockey. That figure there didn't come in a box. But it *did* come with a defunct battery."

Layla lit up another Virginia Slims, sucked on it until her cheeks caved in, and waved the exhaled smoke around, as if that helped anything.

"Who in the world collects *batteries?*" I asked.

"People are nuts," Layla said, and tapped her noggin, as if providing a visual demonstration of the fact. "They'll collect anything that's rare. You see, that battery was *recalled*, so finding a figurine with the original crappy battery still inside is like unearthing a new Mona Lisa, if you know what I mean."

"So...the twenty grand reward. It's not for the *figurine*. It's for the *battery*."

"Bingo, kid. Well, I mean, it's for both. The matched set. You see, one without the other ain't worth diddly squat."

My heart sunk. "So, how much are we talking about, here? For the figurine without the battery?"

"*Look* at it," Layla said, and jabbed a cigarette at the little guy on the toilet. "They made thousands of 'em. What do *you* think it's worth?"

"A thousand bucks?"

"Not even a thousand pennies."

I did the math as I shot Doo-Doo Daddy a dirty look. Ten bucks! Geeze! Twice that blasted thing had nearly gotten me in a heap of trouble with Tom. Now it had just dashed all my hopes with a single grunt from its brand-new battery.

I reached for the door handle.

"Sorry to have bothered you," I said, and opened the door. Then a thought hit me. "Hey, wait a minute! Layla, what does the original battery look like?"

"I'm not sure. I only saw it once. Brown, I think."

My gut flopped. "Hold on a second. Let me make a call."

The old lady sucked on a cigarette and eyed me like a dehydrated chameleon as I dialed Winky's number. He picked up on the first ring.

"Winky!"

"Yeah. Hey there, Val Pa –"

"Listen! Do you still have that battery you took out of that figurine the other day?"

"Yeah. I think so."

For the second time in as many days, I could have kissed Walter J. Winchley.

"Hold onto it. I'll be there in ten minutes!"

I hung up and looked at Layla. She was staring at me, open mouthed, her cigarette dangling off her lip like a miniature, gut-sprung diving board.

"Don't tell me!" she gasped.

"Yes! But I've got to hurry. Stay here. I'll be back in ten minutes. Fifteen, tops."

Chapter Twenty-Six

Why is it that whenever you're in a hurry, the world seems to delight in throwing obstacles in your path?

I rumbled down Gulf Boulevard at the incredible pace of twenty-three miles per hour, stuck in the right lane behind a stupid garbage truck. Not only was it slow, it stunk to high heaven in the late-summer heat.

I couldn't pass, because a Buick with Jersey plates was tagging along in the left lane, a car length behind the truck. Finally, it got into a turn lane. I maneuvered over into the left lane and whizzed by the stinking garbage scow. As I passed, I shot the truck driver a dirty look, then realized I was almost at the corner where I needed to make a right turn.

Oops!

I swerved into the lane in front of the truck, hit my blinker and my brakes, and took a hairpin right onto First Street East toward Sunset Beach.

I could still hear the garbage truck's horn resounding in my ears when, a few minutes later, I roared up to Winky's Donut Shop and slammed on the brakes.

"Winky!" I yelled. I stumbled out of the car and nearly tripped on my mad dash to get to the donut shop's service window.

"Hey there!" Winky said. "You want a cup of coffee? It's on the house. Or should I say, on the shop?"

Winky chortled at his own joke. I didn't.

"No thanks. Listen, where's that battery I called you about?"

Winky's face went quizzical. He looked to his left and grunted in a way that made me wonder if he'd just broken something inside his brain that was essential for higher thought.

"Come on, Winky. I don't have a lot of time."

"Wait a minute!" Winky hollered, as if a light had just flicked on in the back porch of his mind. "Is that *you*, Val?"

"Of course it's me!"

Just then, I caught the reflection of myself in the window pane and remembered I was dressed like a country-western disco flooze-bag.

Winky whistled and shook his head. "Well I'll be darned. I knowed times was tough, but –"

"Ugh! Winky, I don't have time to explain right now. Where's that battery I called you about?"

"Well, it's over yonder." Winky pointed back behind me.

"What do you mean?"

"I'm fairly sure it's still in that there dumpster. They hat'n come and dumped it yet. You can see fer yoreself, Val. It's plum full-up to the brim."

I looked over at the dumpster, then down at my outfit. The only way I could get any trashier was to crawl inside a garbage container.

Nice one, universe.

I unzipped my platform boots and kicked them off. Then I made a dash across the lot to the dumpster, took a long, deep breath, and climbed up its rusty metal side.

The odor coming off its contents would have curled my hair, if it hadn't been made of polyester. I hadn't smelled anything that bad since my Aunt Pansy cooked collard greens and chit'lin's together in the same pot.

I swung a leg over and straddled the dented metal rim of the mustard-colored dumpster. Cautiously, I took a tentative step onto a cardboard box. It gave way, and I tumbled head-first into the belly of the foul-smelling beast.

If I'd have been Jonah, I'd have given that halitosis-ridden whale a breath mint the size of a Buick.

The stench made my jaw clamp tighter than a girdle on a pregnant rhinoceros. If I was going to survive this, I was going to have to breathe through an orifice that didn't have olfactory sensors.

What would Valiant Stranger do?

With no handy gas mask to avail myself of, I closed my eyes and thought of kittens playing with balls of string. Then I shut off my nostrils, opened my mouth, and got to work.

The first bag I tore into contained the remains of some kid's beach birthday party, complete with frosting-smeared Spongebob plates and half a dozen dirty diapers.

Ugh!

If that wasn't disgusting enough, when I opened the second bag, I hit the motherlode – of putrefied fish heads and guts.

"Arrggh!"

I screamed and flung the fishy bag out of the dumpster. After that, things got a little blurry. As I continued to rifle through the rest of the mountain of garbage bags, I guess I began to suffer from PTSD...putrid trash shock dementia....

As fate would have it, inside that horrid dumpster of iniquity I found everything *but* salvation. Like a rabid dog, I was tearing open one of the last garbage bags left when Winky's head popped up over the rim of the dumpster.

"Val, you got to get yourself outta there!"

"I'm almost done..."

"I mean *now*, girl! The garbage guys are here!"

"No!" I screeched, and popped my head up for a look. I was so shocked I forgot and breathed through my nose.

Ugh!

Glaring at me was the same brawny guy I'd sped passed on Gulf Boulevard...and then slammed on my brakes.

I smiled weakly at the garbage truck driver.

"Look, sir," I said, "all I need is like...five minutes more. Can't you just skip this dumpster for now?"

"Not on your life," he said. "That dumpster's private property. Get out now or I'm calling the cops."

Great. That was the absolute last thing I needed. If one of Tom's buddies showed up...well, I didn't want to think about it.

Defeated, I climbed out of the dumpster and watched, in no-longer-sparkly hot-pants, as the garbage truck hoisted the dumpster into the air. The car-sized container swung softly, like a Ferris wheel cage, then flipped over. Mounds of smelly garbage tumbled into the truck's waiting bed...

...along with a twenty-thousand dollar battery and my best Dolly Parton wig.

Chapter Twenty-Seven

"And then what happened?" Laverne asked, hanging on my every word.

We were in her kitchen and my Destiny was a gonner.

I'd arrived home looking, smelling and feeling like a pole cat stuck in a sewage treatment plant. I'd stripped off naked in the garage and thrown my hot pants, halter and the rest of Destiny into the garbage bin.

I'd just finished showering with Lifebuoy and Clorox when Laverne had called me, wanting to talk face-to-face.

She'd said it was urgent, so I'd thrown on some comfy clothes and dropped over, my hair still damp and smelling faintly of Ty-D-Bol. One look at me and she'd told me to tell my story first.

"Then I had to call Layla and give her the bad news, Laverne. The battery's gone forever."

Laverne cocked her horsey head and frowned. "Oh, honey, I'm sorry about that."

I sipped a cup of brown liquid Laverne had said was coffee, and glanced around at the veritable army of Vegas memorabilia crammed in every nook and cranny of her place. A shiny Frank Sinatra figurine smirked and winked a holographic blue eye at me, amplifying my suspicion that every joke ever played in the world was somehow on me.

I set down my cup and picked up Doo-Doo Daddy. I'd brought him along for dramatic effect. I slammed the ugly lump of porcelain on the counter and threw my arms up in frustration.

"I don't *get* it, Laverne. What kind of *idiot* would waste money on stupid crap like that?"

"I sure don't know, honey."

Laverne took my hand and offered me a kind, sympathetic smile. All around her, from every bookshelf, countertop and window ledge, hordes of diminutive figures mirrored her expression with their painted-on lips and eyes.

My cheeks flamed from the unintentional insult I'd just hurled. But fortunately, my poison dart had flown right over Laverne's head. Her kindly smile never missed a beat.

I cleared my throat and shifted my gaze back to the hideous figurine on the counter.

"Right. So, when I called her back, Layla told me she'd give me ten bucks for it. But I tell you, Laverne, it's worth more than that to me to be able to smash his crappy little brains in for making me climb in that dumpster!"

Laverne pursed her lips and touched my forearm.

"By the way," I said, "you wouldn't happen to have a hammer I could borrow, would you?"

Laverne bit her lip. "What about your bet with Tom?"

"I just lost *twenty grand*, Laverne. Losing my bet with Tom is *nothing* compared to that."

Laverne burst into tears.

Shocked by her unexpected response, I nearly missed catching her when she fell into my arms. I held her awkwardly as she sobbed into my shoulder.

"Geeze, Laverne. I'm sorry. It's just that…. Okay. I won't smash it. Stop crying, okay?"

"Oh, it's not that," she sobbed.

"What is it, then? J.D. troubles?"

Laverne pulled away and sniffed. "No. Well...yes. But that's not it either."

"Tell me, Laverne. What's bothering you?"

"Oh, Val! I did something horrible back when I was in Vegas! I thought the past was behind me. But then, last night...it finally caught up with me!"

"Geeze, Laverne! What did you do?"

"Here. Read this." Laverne jabbed a letter toward me. "It came in the mail yesterday."

I unfolded the letter and read it while Laverne sniffed back tears and gnawed at her red-lacquered nails.

DEAR MS. LAVERNE VIVIAN Cowens,

It has come to our attention that while living in Las Vegas, Nevada, you failed to perform your sworn allegiance as an upstanding citizen of these blessed United States of America.

For all intents and purposes, Ms. Cowens, you have stolen an artifact that belongs rightfully to all of your fellow Americans, and one that should have been available to them through the public domain.

Attached, please find evidentiary substantiation of said offence.

I flipped to the next page. It was a bad photocopy of a lending card from the Clark County Library for a book entitled, *How to Get Blood Stains Out of Anything.*

Laverne had checked it out in 1999.

I flipped back to the letter, my ears already heating up like a small furnace explosion.

Ms. Cowens, we know that the idea of any criminal proceedings being filed against you must come as a shock. But, thankfully, there is a way you can expunge potential charges and keep your good name in full standing.

Simply enclose a check for fines and filing charges of $89.94 and we will act as your fiduciary representative, handle all further governmental inquiries, and send you a receipt of final outcome, clearing you of any criminal activities in this matter.

Sincerely,

Ferrol Finkerman

Attorney at Law

P.S. Send your check within the next 24 hours and receive a $3.25 discount!

P.S.S. If you have any questions regarding the above matter, you may consult our offices for the reasonable fee of $250 per hour.

I folded the letter and handed it back to Laverne.

"Is it as bad as I thought?" Laverne asked.

"It's worse," I said through gritted teeth. "But not for you. For Ferrol ratfink Finkerman."

I tapped a finger on the countertop. "Laverne, I think it's high time we hired a hitman."

Laverne sniffed and nodded solemnly.

"Okay, Val. I'll go get my rolodex."

Chapter Twenty-Eight

Like my three ex-husbands, Ferrol Finkerman had gone and gotten on my last nerve.

His extortion letter to Laverne had worn out the last threads on his Southern welcome mat. Whatever grace I'd allowed him in the past was now as null and void as my Baptist starter-marriage.

I sat at my desk with my cellphone in my hand. As my index finger poised over the last digit in his phone number, I had to admit that over the years, Finkerman had proven to be a worthy adversary.

Only one other person in my life had been able to get my goat like Finkerman. Her name, of course, was Lucille Jolly-Short.

My adoptive mother held a mysterious power over me that could send me into a conniption fit at her beck and call. Like the most maniacal of evil geniuses, Lucille could make me feel lousy for stuff I didn't even remember doing.

Talking with Mom, even over the phone, was like waking up from a drunken blackout with the dreadful, nagging suspicion I'd robbed a bank, kicked a pastor in the groin, or sold my sister into slavery.

Once trapped in her vortex of guilt, I was powerless to do anything but wince and bide my time, paralyzed with pre-programmed regrets, while Mom's jabs of judgement stabbed my conscience until she'd rendered me totally incapacitated....

By some miracle, I'd survived my early childhood training. So I knew I was prepared – no matter what Finkerman might throw at me.

I tapped the last digit on the cellphone and waited like a spider for him to fall into my trap.

"Thank you for calling the award-winning law offices of Ferrol Finkerman, attorney at law," Fargo Finkerman said.

"Yes. Hello. I'd like to speak with Mr. Finkerman."

"May I ask who's calling?"

"Val Fremden."

Fargo snickered, slightly unnerving me.

"Just a moment," he said.

I waited on the line for at least a minute while a fly crawled across the kitchen window pane. I wished the fly was Finkerman, and I was a flyswatter.

"Val Fremden," Finkerman's voice came on the line, making me jump.

"Ferrol Finkerman," I said sourly.

"Oh, come now. No need for attitude. What say we get together for a little tit for tat. You show me yours, I show you mine."

"Could you come up with an analogy that doesn't make me want to hurl my lunch?"

"Always the joker. Well, this time, the jokes on you."

"I wouldn't count on it."

"What say we meet at my office and find out?"

"Fine. What time?"

"Does *now* work for you?"

"As my mother always says, 'There's no time like the present to wipe a smile off someone's face.'"

I RANG THE DOORBELL and waited.

"Be right there," Laverne's voice called out.

From the bushes beside her front door, two gnomes stared at me, their faces ecstatic with glee at the prospect of heading off to work with a hammer and a shovel.

I want that hammer.

The door flew open.

"What's up?" Laverne asked.

"I need to borrow that letter," I said. "The one from Finkerman."

"Sure, honey. Do you want to meet Harvey Hooters?"

"Who?"

"Harvey Hooters. The hitman."

"You're joking."

"Not a whit. He said he could snuff Finkerman out, no problem."

"You actually hired a hitman?"

"Of course. That's what you told me to do, isn't it?"

"Geeze, Laverne! And *Harvey Hooters?* I can't say that's the kind of name that instills fear into the hearts of men."

Laverne cocked her head sideways. "Is it supposed to?"

I took the letter from her hand, then sucked in a deep breath to calm myself.

"Listen, Laverne, how about, just for the moment, we consider this Harvey Hooters guy as Plan B."

"I think it's too late for that, Val. By the way, did you get my kosher water?"

Chapter Twenty-Nine

I pulled up in front of Finkerman's office and grabbed my dossier of evidence. It consisted of the cellphone pictures of Finkerman at Walmart and the extortion letter he'd slapped Laverne with for an overdue book.

Having failed to secure Goober's dreamcatcher with stealth and a blonde wig as big as a beach cooler, I was back, this time in more normal attire, to initiate a couple of trades. If all went according to plan, I'd swap the incriminating photos for the dreamcatcher, and the incriminating letter – along with a threat to report Finkerman to the bar for extortion – in exchange for him dropping his suit against me for the incident involving Laverne's gastronomically disastrous cookies.

I climbed out of Maggie and marched to Finkerman's door in full Valiant Stranger mode.

It's time for that frizzy-haired freak to take a fall.

"Ms. Fremden, I presume?" young Fargo Finkerman said when I walked in the door. His face and voice mirrored his uncle's uncanny ability for smarm.

"Yes," I answered.

Fargo mashed a button on his phone. I heard a buzz emanate from behind Finkerman's office door. A moment later, the door cracked open and Ferrol Finkerman's pointy, Pinocchio nose poked out.

"You look different today," he said. "Do come in."

I followed Finkerman into his office and sat down in a fake leather chair that was sticky to the touch. I shivered with disgust. I needed to get out of there before I caught an STD, so I cut right to the chase.

"I think you have something of mine, Finkerman, and I'd like to get it back."

Finkerman looked surprised. "*I've* got something of *yours?*"

"Yes. A...redneck dreamcatcher."

Finkerman laughed for a full minute while I visualized taking another shower in bleach...and pouring some down his throat while I was at it.

"That's priceless," he said finally, trying to compose himself. "And, pray tell, what does this 'redneck dreamcatcher' of yours look like?"

"You know good and well what it looks like."

Finkerman wiped tears from his eyes. "Well, to be honest, I had no idea of its ethnic origins when I bought it."

I unclenched my vice-like jaws long enough to hiss, "Just hand it over, Finkerman, and I'll give you something in return."

"Hmmm," Finkerman hummed. He folded his hands into a steeple and touched the tip to his lips.

"So *that's* why you dropped by unannounced yesterday."

I nearly swallowed my tonsils.

"What are you talking about?"

"Grow up, Fremden. I've got this place covered with surveillance cameras." He pointed to one in the corner. "I've got your whole act down on tape. Nicely done, by the way, Ms. *Feldman.*"

"But...how did you know it was *me?*"

"I'd recognize that big butt of yours from a mile away. *Without* binoculars, I might add."

"Okay. Fine. It was me. Now what do you want for it?"

"The tape, or the dreamcatcher?"

I groaned inside. "Both."

"How about let's say...five hundred bucks."

"Five hundred...ugh!"

I dug around in my purse and pulled out my cellphone.

"How about *this* instead!"

I shoved the phone screen into Finkerman's smug face. Reflecting back in his bugged-out eyes was a clear shot of him paying a Walmart cashier for a three-pack of Fruit-of-the-Looms. The darkened area on the back of his pants was irrefutable proof he was in desperate need of a change of undies, and pronto.

Finkerman's expression went all twitchy. He chewed his bottom lip while his face turned the color of a honey-baked ham.

Finally, he blew out a breath and said, "Deal. The last thing I need is for clients to know I shop at Walmart."

He reached in a desk drawer and handed over the video tape. I deleted the photo from my phone.

"So, where's the dreamcatcher?" I asked.

"That's a little more complicated."

"What do you mean?"

"Well, you see, on my way back to my Hummer, some guy at the yard sale offered to trade me for it. What can I say? I'm an old softie. Besides, I needed a radio and a potato peeler more than *that* stupid thing."

My heart sunk.

Oh crap!

"Geeze, Finkerman! What'd the guy look like?"

"I dunno."

"Think! It's important."

"Just your average white guy. Tall. Slim. Cheezy moustache."

Goober!

"Was he bald?"

Finkerman shrugged. "Hard to tell. He was wearing a baseball cap."

I slumped back in my seat. Finkerman grinned at me like a *Chucky* doll.

"If it's any consolation," he smirked, "you can have the potato peel-er."

Chapter Thirty

"So, that leaves us with the little matter of my defamation suit against you," Finkerman said, and leaned back in his chair.

I took a deep breath, trying to recover from the reeling blow that Finkerman had traded away Goober's dreamcatcher, and that there was barely a chance in hell I'd ever see it again.

I sat up and peeled my left forearm off the armrest of the sticky vinyl chair. I wished I'd been wearing long sleeves, pants and boots...instead of a short jean skirt and sleeveless pink tank top. Every inch of my exposed skin crawled at the prospect of making contact with any surface in his office.

"Not exactly, Finkerman. I've got another bone to pick with you."

"Really? And what would that be?"

"This."

I shoved Finkerman's letter to Laverne across the desk at him.

"As far as I can remember," I said, "extortion is still illegal in these, and I quote, 'blessed United States of America.'"

Finkerman snatched up the letter, looked it over and smiled proudly at his handiwork.

"Ah, yes. Cowens. She's that wacko neighbor of yours from the yard sale, right? I have to say, I'd never seen an Armani suit in size munchkin before."

"Leave her alone!" I yelled. "What you're doing is extortion! What kind of creep takes advantage of senior citizens? And give up the lawsuit against me, Finkerman, or I'm reporting you to the Florida Bar Association!"

Finkerman mulled over the idea. "And if I do give it up?"

I nodded at the letter in his hand. "I'll pretend I never saw that."

"Saw what?" Finkerman asked, and ripped the letter in half.

I gasped. "Don't you dare!"

"Dare what?" Finkerman asked, and ripped it in half again.

"I'll sue you!" I screeched.

"For what?" Finkerman laughed.

"For being a bona fide fleabag!" I yelled, and catapulted across his desk.

I grabbed his spidery wrist and arm-wrestled him for the letter. As I tangoed around on my knees on his credenza, he managed to mash a buzzer on his phone. A second later, young Fargo Finkerman dashed in.

"Help me, you dolt!" Finkerman bellowed.

Fargo took a tentative step toward us.

"Touch me and I'll sue you!" I hissed.

The young man shrunk back, uncertainty marring his face like a bad tattoo.

"Come on, Finkerman," I grunted, getting him in a headlock. "Give me the letter. If there's nothing illegal about it, why do you care if I have it or not?"

"Watch the hair!" Finkerman yelped. "Tell me the secret ingredient in those nasty cookies of yours and I'll think about letting you have the letter back."

"No!"

I grabbed for the wad of torn paper in his hand and missed.

"Come on," Finkerman said, pushing my arm away. "What was in those cookies? Let me guess. *Insecticide?*"

"No!" I grunted. "If it was, you'd be dead by now, you blood-sucking cockroach!"

"Um...should I call the police?" Fargo asked, and for a moment stopped wringing his hands.

"No!" Finkerman and I yelled in unison.

The unexpected point of agreement made us both stop cold. We stared at each other in an unspoken détente, and eased up on our battlefield positions.

"It appears we have reached a stalemate," Finkerman said, and carefully smoothed his thin, frizzy hair with a wobbly hand.

"Looks like," I grumbled.

Fargo smiled like a bank hostage and asked, "Coffee, anyone?"

Chapter Thirty-One

G *reat. I was batting zero.*

No dreamcatcher. No extortion letter. One still-active lawsuit against me.

I'd played my best hand against Finkerman and come away with zilch.

Adding insult to injury, I could still picture the shyster's smug face as I'd walked out the door. He'd smiled like a catfish with gas and waved goodbye at me with a fistful of Laverne's shredded letter raining down in bits onto the sidewalk.

As I'd strapped myself into Maggie to make my getaway, the sore winner had gloated with glee, and informed me that possession was nine-tenths of the law.

I'd un-gleefully informed *him* that he was nine-tenths of a scumbag.

It was all too much. I snapped. On the way home, I stopped at ACE Hardware off Boca Ciega Drive and bought myself a hammer. It was an act of self-preservation. I was literally trembling with rage, and didn't trust myself to be able to safely climb the ladder to get up into my attic.

"MY LIFE'S GOING DOWN the toilet because of *you!*" I hissed at the hapless lump of ceramic shaped like a fat man on a crapper.

I must have been blinded by anger, because the irony of my statement completely escaped me.

Perched alone on a concrete block out in the backyard, the Dr. Dingbat's Difficult Defecation figurine looked rather small and defenseless. As the figurine's lone judge, jury and executioner, I became a bit unnerved when I noticed that its grimacing expression had appeared to shift. Somehow, it now looked more like a plea for mercy than an effort to dislodge excrement.

But there was no turning back. The Hammer of Justice had spoken.

I raised the shiny new hammer over my headful of rationalizations.

True, there'd been no trial. But the death sentence I'm about to hand down is guaranteed to be swift and merciful....

As the stainless steel hammer impacted his sweaty bald head, Doo-Doo Daddy exploded into a million pieces. He also let loose a slow, pathetic groan that reverberated off the wall of the house like a warped Bob Dylan song played at too slow a speed.

The relief was instant.

Ridding the world of one more hideous creation from the sick mind of mankind was a life purpose I had embraced since my twenties. It never failed to soothe whatever ailed me.

Scintillating satisfaction surged through me as I stared down at the results of my handiwork. One blow from my Hammer of Justice had vanquished the vile, villainous foe forever. All that remained was a scattered pile of shards...and, oddly, a little speaker-thingy attached to a battery by a bit of bent wire.

I picked up the strange innards. It let out one last mournful grunt and dislodged a little slip of paper with the words NIM 1 printed on it.

I pictured poor little NIM 1, and all the other NIMs out there, slaving away as underpaid inspectors in some Chinese sweat-shop, wasting day after mindless day quality-checking an endless factory line of fat, sweaty, little white men grunting on porcelain thrones.

I tossed the noisemaker thingy back on the ground.

Compared to NIM 1, maybe my life wasn't so bad after all.

I'D LOST MY BET WITH Tom, but it had been worth it. However, as I swept up the broken remains of Dr. Dingbat's disgrace to mankind, a sneaky second thought crept into my endorphin-filled brain.

If a figurine shatters in a backyard and no one else is around to hear it, does it still make a sound? Does it still count as a deal-breaker?

"Val? Is that you?"

I whirled around. Laverne was at the picket fence that separated our yards. I hid the hammer behind my back.

"Uh...hey, Laverne."

"How did it go with the letter?" she asked.

"Not great."

Laverne bit her bottom lip. "Does this mean I'm gonna lose my good name, Val?"

"No, Laverne. Not if I can help it."

"So, what do we do now?"

My fingers wrapped tighter around the handle of the shiny new Hammer of Justice, II.

"Well, Laverne, I think it just may be time to initiate Plan B."

Chapter Thirty-Two

Good thing it's garbage day tomorrow.

The bag containing the shattered remains of Doo-Doo Daddy made a dull tinkling sound when I set it on top of the bin in my garage. I hit the remote to raise the garage door, and strolled nonchalantly down the driveway to the sidewalk.

My reconnaissance mission yielded two results.

First, to my delight, my neighbor Jake had already put his trash can out on the curb. It was only 5:45 p.m., making it a risky move, considering it could earn him the wrath of Nancy Bristol-Butt Meyers. She preferred people to wait until after 7 p.m.

Second, to my further delight, no one else was around.

I hurried back into the garage and grabbed the sack of figurine shards. If I put them in Jake's can, there'd be no risk of Tom finding them.

I looked both ways before double-crossing my boyfriend, and scurried over to Jake's trash bin. As I lifted the lid, a Jersey voice sounded behind me.

"What'cha doin', Val?"

My back arched. I turned around slowly.

"Uh...hi, Jake. Our bin is full...I hope you don't mind?"

"Nah. Anytime."

"Thanks."

I dropped the bag of incriminating evidence inside the can and closed the lid.

"So, how's the writing biz treatin' ya?" Jake asked, and scratched a mosquito bite on his hairy arm with his hairy hand.

"All I can say is, 'Thank God Tom's got a steady job.'"

Jake laughed.

I nodded toward the sign in his yard.

"So, how's it going with *your* venture?"

"You mean You're in Charge? Eh. It has its ups and downs. Speaking of which...."

Jake nodded at something behind me. I turned to see Nancy Meyers marching toward us, a slip of paper in her tight little fist.

"Johnson!" she barked as she descended upon us. "How many times do I have to tell you? Garbage bins are unsightly, and shouldn't be on the street before seven!"

"Some things shouldn't be on the street *ever*," Jake whispered in my ear.

"What was that?" Nancy said. "If you have something to say, say it to *all* of us."

Jake smiled. "I was just wondering if you're enjoying your 'You're in Charge' mug?"

"Oh. Well, yes."

"Would you like another? You know, for a matching set?"

Nancy's hard face softened slightly. "Yes. I think Ralph would like that."

"Hold on, and I'll fetch you one."

"Jake, could I have one, too?" I asked.

"Sure! Be right back."

As Jake disappeared into the house, Nancy turned her attention to *my* shortcomings...or, to be more specific, my potential *future* shortcomings.

"Fremden, I hear you're getting a dog on Saturday."

"How did you...yes."

"Wait here. You need a copy of the neighborhood handbook I prepared on dog etiquette."

Nancy trotted back across the street and disappeared inside her house. Jake came out of his garage, toting two "You're In Charge" mugs full of hot, black coffee.

"Where'd the Knick Knack Nazi go?" he asked.

"To gather her propaganda. She'll be back in a minute."

"Good. I wouldn't want her to miss out on another cup of my special brew."

"Jake! You didn't!"

He grinned like a happy chimp. "I did."

"Not both, I hope."

Jake appeared taken aback. "No. I am not an animal!"

I laughed. "So, which one has the special sauce?"

"The one in my left hand."

"Are you sure?"

"I'm positive. I never mess up when I'm slipping someone a Mickie. Had lots of practice in the joint, you know."

"No. I didn't know."

Jake's eyes darted to the left. "Here she comes. Take this one."

He handed me the mug in his right hand and beamed a prison smile at Nancy.

"Here you go, Ms. Meyers. I took the liberty of filling your cup with coffee."

Nancy grabbed the mug. "Thank you. You *do* make good coffee, Jake Johnson, I'll give you that. But that doesn't excuse you from breaking the rules."

Nancy slapped a laminated card in his hand. "Here's another schedule outlining appropriate times for garbage bins, lawn watering, and the like."

She shook her finger at him. "No more excuses!"

"Yes, ma'am," Jake said.

"And as for you, Fremden, here's the dog etiquette guide. Read it. Know it. Live it."

She handed me a booklet and took a sip from her mug. The right side of Jake's mouth twitched into something between a grimace and a smile.

"So, I need to get back," Nancy said. "I'm in the middle of cooking dinner. Good evening to you both. And remember, *follow the rules!*"

We nodded and watched her walk away.

"I wonder what she's cooking," I said when she was out of earshot.

"Probably cabbage with roasted toddlers," Jake said. "Toddlers *never* follow rules. They're like puppies, that way."

The corner of my upper lip jerked upward at the thought.

"That reminds me. Do you do puppy training?"

"Sure," Jake said. "Just let me know."

"I will."

Jake glanced at Nancy's time schedule in his hand and lifted the bin lid.

"Good thing it's garbage day," he said, and tossed the laminated card inside.

Across the street, I thought I saw Nancy's blinds move.

WITH THE INCRIMINATING shattered figurine evidence safely disposed of, I'd thought my troubles were over – at least for the day.

But I was wrong.

When I went back home and down the hall, I noticed the air was muggy as a swamp.

I looked in my bedroom and gasped.

The window leading to the side yard was wide open. The blinds were a tangled jumble, as if some animal had tried to scale them. Then it dawned on me.

Someone broke in – and left in a hurry!

I must have spooked them!

The hair on the back of my neck stood up. Every drawer in my vanity had been yanked open. They appeared to have been rifled through, too. But I wasn't sure. I wasn't a compulsive neat-nick like Tom.

I opened my jewelry box. It was empty except for a tarnished silver dollar and the pair of fake, five-carat diamond earrings I'd picked up at the Dollar-Store.

Nothing missing. If they weren't after jewelry, what were *they after?*

I turned and saw the folding doors to my closet were pulled back. Panic shot through me.

My shoes!

I scrambled to the closet and grabbed the box that contained the glorious, impossible high heels I'd never wear. I held my breath and opened the box. They were still there.

Whew!

So was the shoebox containing all the old notes and pictures I'd saved of Glad and Tony. Then I noticed a box sitting slightly askew. It was my secret Halloween candy stash. I opened the shoebox. Half of the candy was missing. Someone had stolen all the good stuff!

Dang it! Where am I gonna find chocolate-covered marshmallow ghosts this *time of year?*

I shoved the shoebox full of crappy candy back into place. The box next to it made a chinking sound. I pulled out my secret hoard of figurines and took a look inside.

As far as I could tell, they were all there. Illiterate Giraffe woman. The turd-faced Turtle Boy I'd traded for Tom's football. A World's Greatest Golfer statue, and a pizza baker flipping what I suppose used to be a pizza, but the pie was broken off and missing in action, along with a piece of his hand.

I sighed and put the lid back on the box. As I reached to put it back on the shelf, a thought struck me.

One is missing. The Asian one...Su Mee!

"Finkerman!" I screeched.

The front door opened and slammed closed.

I nearly swallowed my tongue.

The robbers! They're still here!

I panicked, lost my balance, and fell face-first into the closet. My right nostril snagged a shirt button. My right hand managed to catch hold of a coat-hanger. I didn't want to make a sound, so I hung onto the shoulder of a long-sleeved shirt and swayed back and forth like a snockered simpleton on a carnival ride.

"Val? You home?"

Tom!

I opened my mouth to scream, "We've been robbed!" But shut it again without uttering a peep.

I can't tell Tom! If I do, he'd find out about my secret stash of figurines. My cover would be blown, and he'd win our bet!

The thought of losing the bet made my eyes bug out.

I'd be stuck with that hideous chair of his forever!

I steeled myself. What's a little break-in compared to being saddled with a plaid Barcalounger for life?

"I'm in here," I called back.

I stumbled to my feet and scrambled like a maniac to put everything back in order, shoving shoeboxes into their places and kicking closed the closet door.

"What 'cha doing?" Tom called from down the hallway.

"Nothing. Be right there."

I sprinted to the window, closed it, and raked my hands over the twisted blinds to straighten them. They weren't cooperating, so I raised them. They looked better, but not great.

"What's for dinner? I'm starving!" Tom called out.

Crap! I hadn't given it a thought...

I scooted over to my vanity and closed all the drawers. I took a step toward the door, then turned back and re-opened two of the drawers. I left them ajar so Tom wouldn't get suspicious.

The ding of the microwave timer echoed down the hallway. I padded to the kitchen just in time to see Tom raise Jake's "You're in Charge" mugful of coffee to his lips.

My gut churned.

Should I say something or not?

Tom was a good guy. But his careless actions of late had cost me Goober's dreamcatcher and, quite possibly, saddled me with the burden of having to look at his disgusting plaid chair until the day I died or it caused me to go blind.

I decided to keep my mouth shut and let karmic justice play its own hand.

I forced a smile as Tom took a sip of coffee.

If Tom's actions had been well intentioned, he was innocent – and there'd be nothing in that cup but brewed coffee. But if he was guilty of typical male thoughtlessness, Jake would have peed in it. Tom would get his just payback for the chair, for selling Goober's dreamcatcher...and for that stupid vibrator prank.

In fact, the way I saw it, his losing the dreamcatcher exonerated me from smashing Doo-Doo Daddy to bits. I'd been driven beyond distraction, so I deserved a Mulligan.

"This is exceptionally good coffee," Tom said.

"Glad you like it," I said sweetly. "It's something new."

As I watched Tom take another sip, I realized that the chance Jake would have mixed up the mugs – or peed in both of them – was pretty slim.

Still, just to be on the safe side, I opted out of kissing Tom hello.

Chapter Thirty-Three

After Tom left for work Thursday morning, I got busy on the assignment due tonight for my *Mystery Writing for Fun and Profit* class.

Each student was supposed to create a mock crime scene report. But, thanks to the break in yesterday, I didn't have to fake it. My bedroom actually *was* a real, bona fide crime scene.

I printed off the checklist that Langsbury had emailed us, filled it out, and examined the resulting document.

Crime Scene Checklist:

Victim: Me.

Nature of Crime: Theft

Property Damage: One mangled mini-blind.

Object(s) Stolen or Reported Missing: One tacky "Su Mee" figurine. A bunch of marshmallow Halloween ghosts in individual black-and-orange wrappers. My sense of security.

Possible Motive(s): Hunger? Bad Taste? Insanity? Revenge?

Possible Suspects: Dirtbag attorney. Voracious hobo. Teenage mutant. Escaped circus animal.

Action Steps: Search internet for marshmallow ghosts for sale. Spray-paint obscenities on yellow Hummer. Hire Harvey Hooters the hitman to break Finkerman's stupid, Pinocchio nose.

I sighed and flung the paper onto my desk. There was no way I could hand it in. No one would ever believe it.

I went back to the scene of the crime – my bedroom closet – and reexamined all the shoeboxes. After checking through about thirty of them, I discovered a pair of sandals I'd forgotten I'd bought. But as far as I could tell, nothing else was missing.

Weird. Who would break in just to take candy and a figurine?

The whole thing could have been the work of some bored teenager. But why would they have taken only *one* of the figurines? And why *Su Mee?*

Maybe I'd interrupted the intruder before they could find what they were really looking for.

Or maybe I hadn't.

Assuming the perpetrator got what they'd come for, the obvious culprit was Finkerman. He'd given me Su Mee in exchange for Laverne's toxic cookies. Now he was bent on revenge for the bad trade. He'd stooped to breaking and entering. But, then again, I'd stooped to breaking wind and diarrhea....

Maybe it really is *time for Plan B.*

I walked back into my office and picked up my Crime Scene Checklist. I wadded the paper up, tossed it into the trash, and wondered what a real, live hitman actually looked like.

I WAS IN THE GARAGE, stuffing my incriminating Crime Scene Checklist into the garbage bin when I started hearing voices. Thankfully, my garage door was open, and the voices belonged to my neighbors Jake and Nancy.

"Ralph's a thief!" I heard Nancy say. "And he's getting worse in his old age. I need to do something about him, Jake. It's gotten to where I can't leave anything unlocked. My brooch my grandmother gave me is missing, and he won't tell me where he put it. I need your help."

"What can I do about it?" Jake asked.

"Talk to him. Maybe he'll listen to you."

"Why me?"

"You understand the criminal mind," Nancy said. "You've been in the...uh...you've been incarcerated. Right?"

"Yes. But that doesn't make me a psychologist for the criminally insane."

"Please," Nancy pleaded, her voice softening. "At least meet him. Maybe he'll tell you what he did with my jewelry."

"Ugh. Okay."

I saw Jake's hairy arm come into view around the corner of his house. Instinct took over, and I ducked behind my trash can. I peeked around the bin and saw Nancy tugging Jake by the hand into her house.

What in the world is going on?

I stood up. The blinds in Nancy's front window angled closed.

*Is Jake being set up? Oh my lord! What if this is some kind of...*man trap? *No one's ever seen Ralph. Maybe he died and Nancy needs a new victim!*

I walked to the end of my driveway and looked around. The coast was clear, so I did the only thing I could think of. I ran across the street to Nancy's house, snuck up beside her front window and put an ear to the pane.

Nothing.

I snuck around to the side of the house and tried my luck at a window lined with empty terracotta pots. I couldn't believe my ear.

"Tell him what you did with my brooch," I heard Nancy say.

A man laughed. It didn't sound like Jake, but then again, I'd never heard him laugh under duress.

"Tell him!" Nancy screeched.

"Never! You're crazy!" a man said. The voice was definitely not Jake's. It had to be Ralph's.

"Do something, Jake," Nancy barked.

"Like what?" Jake said.

"Grab him and hold him down," she said.

"Not on your life!" Ralph said.

"He's a huge guy," Jake said. "I don't want to get on his bad side. He could hurt me!"

"Coward!" Nancy spat.

I leaned over for better acoustics and knocked over one of the empty terracotta pots.

"What was that?" Nancy asked.

I didn't stick around for Jake's reply. I scrambled out of Nancy's yard and across the road faster than an Olympic sprinter riding a rocket. I skipped by my garbage bin, hit the remote on the garage door, and high-tailed it into my house, my heart pounding in my throat.

I gulped down a few breaths, then peeked through my front blinds. Nancy's binoculars were trained on me.

I jerked my hand away from the blinds. My legs felt as wobbly as boiled spaghetti. I took a step and collapsed into Tom's old chair. As I sat there waiting to regain use of my limbs, I wondered what kind of weird stuff was going on behind closed doors in my neighborhood...

...and how in the world was Tom's ugly chair so darn comfortable?

"WELL, IT'S ALL ARRANGED. Harvey's gonna meet us after class tonight," Laverne said as she climbed into Maggie's passenger seat.

"Are you sure we should involve him?" I asked, regretting my agreement to the deal we'd struck earlier in the day.

"Like you said, Val, Finkerman's left us no choice."

"Well, I wouldn't go *that* far."

Laverne's smooth, penciled-on eyebrows turned lumpy as she furrowed her brow.

"Val, I'm not gonna have my headstone read, 'Here lies Laverne Cowens, liar and thief of Clark County.'"

"I doubt an overdue library book would ever lead to *that*."

"Maybe not. But I don't want him running your name through the mud, either. You know you're like the daughter I never had, don't you?"

"Thanks, Laverne."

And you're like the crazy, loveable, air-headed aunt I never had.

Laverne reached for her seatbelt. "What exactly did you do to rile up Finkerman, anyway, Val?"

"Well, at the yard sale, I...."

...gave him your deadly cookies! I can't tell her that!

"I...I called him a scumbag. Or, more accurately, nine-tenths of one."

Laverne nodded and pursed her thin lips.

"I understand, honey. In Vegas, they got a saying about people like him."

"What's that, Laverne?"

The old woman turned and smiled at me brightly.

"If the scumbag fits, put it over his head until he stops breathing."

Chapter Thirty-Four

"So you're telling me *no one* did the crime scene assignment for last week?" Angela Lansgsbury asked.

Exasperated, she grabbed a pencil and started digging at her scalp. She eyed us, her three remaining students, as if we'd just committed a felony.

"No ma'am," we all mumbled.

Langsbury's efforts loosened a few flakes of dandruff. They tumbled to her shoulders as she reemployed the pencil as a pointer. She jabbed it at Clarice and started to say something, but then the old woman appeared to lose steam. Her thin, translucent arms fell to her sides and she let out a huge sigh.

"Okay," she said. "How about we just do a Q and A instead. You gals got any questions?"

"About what?" Clarice asked, her cheeks nearly matching her auburn hair.

"About *writing?*" Langsbury said. Her face appeared as weary and lifeless as a worn-out ragdoll. "Perhaps a plot point you're stuck on?"

"Oh," Clarice said, her eyes trained on her desk. "No."

The yellow, No. 2 writing utensil jabbed my way next. "You, Fremden. You have a question?"

I fidgeted in my desk chair. "Uh...okay. How would you go about locating something that was lost?"

"We need more specifics. What was lost?"

A tacky figurine, a pile of marshmallow ghosts and a redneck dream-catcher made of beer cans, fishing line and a hot-pink pair of panties.

"Let's just say it was a sentimental item," I said.

"How was it lost?"

"At a yard sale. Accidently...uh...traded to an unknown individual for a potato peeler."

Langsbury studied me as if I were a strange new form of fungus. "That's pretty specific, Fremden. Did this actually happen?"

I squirmed in my chair. "Well, uh...I have this friend who –"

"Right," Langsbury said, cutting me off. "As far as I can see, there was no real crime committed in that situation."

She stared blankly at us, her face as curdled as buttermilk. "You three obviously lack motivation. So, why don't we talk about something with motivation behind it? How about we discuss...*murder.*"

Victoria, the woman disguised as a librarian, gasped. "Murder!"

Lansbury's papery lips curled sinisterly. "More specifically, a mur-der*er.*"

The old woman set the pencil down on her desk and raised her thin, spidery hands to shoulder level.

"Okay, ladies. I want you to let go of your *thoughts* and let your *imaginations* take over."

Like a decrepit sorcerer, Langsbury moved her ghostly, tissue-paper hands round and round, as if conjuring an imaginary ball out of thin air.

"Close your eyes and picture the perpetrator in your next story. What does the cad look like? What does he smell like? What are his habits? His daily routine? His longings? His unmet desires? What does he value most?"

Like magic, my mind went blank. Suddenly, out of a mist, a yellow blob emerged. The pulsing yellow amoeba slowly morphed into a Hummer, then into the ghastly, smirking face of Ferrol Finkerman.

Langsbury snapped her fingers. I emerged from my foggy vision.

"So, have you got a villain in mind for your next story?" she asked us.

"Yes," we muttered like hypnotized zombies.

"Can you visualize him?" she asked, and shot a look toward Clarice.

"Most definitely," she answered.

"Is he despicable?"

"Yes!" Victoria said.

Langsbury turned to me. "And how do you *feel* about *your* villain, Fremden?"

"The mere thought of him makes me want to tear my hair out!"

Langsbury smiled. "Good. Now *think*, ladies. About *motivation*. What does your despicable character value above all things?"

"I dunno," Victoria said.

Her hesitant answer broke the magical flow of our instructor's spell, and we returned to hard-slog reality.

Langsbury sighed. "Come on, gals. He's just a *man*. All men value pretty much the same things."

"Like what?" Clarice asked.

Langsbury grinned sadistically. "That's *your* job to decide. Think about it. In fact, let's make that next week's assignment. Drawing out the elements of your perpetrator. Get inside his mind. Uncover his motivation by determining *what he values most*."

Her words caused a lightbulb to go on inside my head.

"I *get it* now," I said, nearly jumping out of my chair. "Thank you Ms. Langsbury! You're...you're *inspirational!*"

The old lady grabbed her pencil and absently jabbed it around in her brown helmet of a hairdo.

"Eh," she shrugged. "I do what I can."

Chapter Thirty-Five

I pulled up along Bimini Circle two houses down from Laverne's place. I cut the lights on Maggie and everything turned a dim, yellowish gray to match the pale light of the streetlamp.

"That's his motorcycle," Laverne whispered, and pointed toward her driveway.

"A Harley? That's not exactly what I'd call a discreet vehicle."

"Harvey said in Florida the more you stand out, the less people notice you."

My lips twisted sourly. "Good point. So, where is he?"

"Right here," a man's voice sounded.

A few inches from the driver's side door, a face loomed at me in the darkness, causing a pathetic little screech to squeak past my tonsils.

"Don't worry," Laverne said, and reached over to pat my hand. "That's Harvey Hooters. You know. The hit man, honey."

"I prefer to be called Double H, or 'The Problem Solver,'" he said, and took a step back from my door.

Even in the dim light, I could see that Harvey had all the outward trappings of a typical Harley biker, including the full beard, the leather vest, the do-rag bandana, and a belly large enough to harbor a full-term manatee fetus.

"Should we go inside to discuss your...*problem?*" Double H asked.

"Sure," Laverne said. "I'll put on a pot of coffee."

She reached down to the floorboard and brought up a plastic container. "I baked brownies in class tonight. They're still warm!"

My gut lurched. "Keep your voices down," I whispered. "Let's get inside before Tom or any of the other nosy neighbors spot us."

Laverne extracted her grasshopper legs from Maggie, and we followed her as she toddled up her driveway. Her silver heels sparkled in the moonlight, giving off the appearance she was stomping on fireflies.

Double H and I took seats at the kitchen counter while Laverne prepared her unintentionally, yet nonetheless malevolent, refreshments.

"Nice place you got here, Laverne," Double H said. "Reminds me of the old times."

"Those were the days, all right," Laverne said.

She looked up at the ceiling dreamily and dumped a scoop of coffee onto the counter, missing the filter by a good six inches.

"So, who is it you want snuffed out?" he asked.

I nearly choked.

"Ferrol Finkerman," Laverne said, as casually as if she were naming him as the recipient for a gift certificate from Sears.

"From what you told me, he sounds like a real jerk," Double H said.

"He does certainly live up to his name," I said.

Double H sucked his teeth. "So, do you have any particular way you want to see him come to his untimely demise?"

"What do you mean?" Laverne asked, and poured water from the carafe into the coffee machine.

"You know," Double H said. "How do you want him done in? Terminated. Murdered."

"Murdered!" Laverne gasped. "Who said anything about *murder?*"

"*You* did," Harvey said. "You said you wanted him snuffed out."

Laverne gulped. "Harvey, I thought that meant you were gonna put snuff up his nose 'til he hollered 'uncle.'"

Double H shook his head and laughed. "I should have known. Laverne, you haven't changed a bit."

"Really, Double H," I said. "We weren't thinking of anything that...you know...*drastic*."

"Maybe you're right," Double H said. "I've seen his type before. Finkerman's a mushroom in the dung pile of life. You get rid of him and another one just sprouts up in his place."

"You are *so* right," I said. "In fact, he's already training someone now. The little toadstool's name is Fargo. He's his nephew."

"I see," Double H said. "So if murder ain't on the agenda, what is?"

"Well, I was thinking," I said. "Tonight, in class, my teacher said that to conquer a villain, first you should try to understand him. You know, what motivates him to do the things he does. She said guys are easy to figure out because they all value the same basic stuff."

Double H grunted and adjusted his do-rag. "Huh. You don't say."

"No, Harvey. Her *teacher* does," Laverne offered, and reached for some coffee cups in the cupboard above her head.

Double H turned his attention back to me, grinning and shaking his bearded head.

"So, anyway, the trick is to find out what Finkerman values most," I explained, "and then use it as leverage to pry Laverne's letter and my lawsuit out of his conniving hands."

"So, how can I help?" Harvey asked.

"Well, you're a man," I said. "What does a man value most?"

"That's easy," he said. "His 'family jewels.'"

I squelched a grimace. "Okay. What else?"

Double H scratched a spot under his do-rag. "Uh...his non-family jewels?"

Well, there went my hopes he was Einstein.

"Okay," I said. "And then?"

"His looks?"

A wheel turned in my rusty mind.

"That's it!" I said. "Let's set up a meeting with Finkerman tomorrow. I think I've got an idea on how we can make him fold."

"Fold what?" Laverne asked.

"His hand," Double H grunted, then nodded like a thug. "All right, then. We'll 'interrogate' him in his office...*get him where he lives.*"

"Exactly!" I said.

A second thought took the wind out of my sails.

"Wait.... Crap!" I said. "We can't. I just remembered. Finkerman's got surveillance cameras all over his office."

Double H shook his head. "I hate when that happens."

Silence fell as the three of us put on our thinking caps. Some fit better than others. As I glanced at the pair beside me, I nearly lost hope. I'd have bet good money that between that pair of dim bulbs, there wasn't twenty watts worth of light shining into the darkness.

"Wait a minute! That's it!" I said, and snapped my fingers.

My partners in crime lifted their sagging heads and eyed me eagerly, as if I held the secret to eternal youth.

I wish.

"What is it?" Laverne asked.

"Finkerman's got surveillance cameras everywhere, right? If we can get our hands on the video tape of him ripping up your letter, we can use it against him. I mean, while I was trying to wrestle your letter from his grubby paws, he practically *confessed* to extortion!"

Double H bobbed his huge lion head. "Works for me."

"I'm in, too," Laverne said, and set two cups of coffee in front of me and Double H.

"Okay, it's settled," I said. "Let's meet back here at seven tomorrow morning."

"But Val, Finkerman's business card said they don't open till nine," Laverne said.

"Precisely," I said with a grin.

Double H returned my smile, and raised a cup of coffee in a toast. "Early morning breaking and entering. I'll drink to that!"

I shot him a small, quick shake of my head and whispered, "I wouldn't if I were you."

Chapter Thirty-Six

Right after Tom left for work, I dashed to the bedroom and pulled out the black shirt and sweatpants I'd stashed in the top drawer of my vanity. In the dusty beams of the morning sun, they suddenly didn't seem like quite the right choice for a daylight robbery.

I should've googled what to wear for such an occasion....

But there was no time for second guessing. I pulled on the sweatpants and t-shirt, and inched my feet into a pair of sporty leather sandals that wouldn't slow me down in case I had to make a run for it.

I decided to leave the black face paint in the drawer.

AS I CROSSED THE LAWN over to Laverne's place, Double H came driving up on his Harley. I wondered how long it would be before my phone buzzed with an alert that SeaWorld was missing a walrus....

This is going to be a disaster.

Double H was dressed in grey chinos, black boots, and a black shirt with red and yellow flames licking up from the bottom hem, giving the appearance he was midway through being burned at the stake.

I turned around, ran back inside my house, thought about giving up on the whole idea, gave up on *that* idea, grabbed a shirt and cap out of Tom's closet, and ran back over to Laverne's.

"Here. Put this on," I said to Double H. I handed him one of Tom's cop shirts. "For a disguise."

"A cop? *That's* a new one," he said as he wriggled into it.

Tom's shirt fit him like a moo-moo on a cow-cow.

I was trying to pull the ends together so he could button it when Laverne came out wearing her gold lame jumpsuit.

Super. Nothing conspicuous about that. Geeze. Maybe the glare shooting off it'll temporarily blind any potential witnesses....

"Laverne, maybe you should stay behind," I said. "If we get caught breaking and entering, you could be charged as an accessory."

Laverne's huge eyes shifted to pleading puppy-dog mode. She shook her armful of bangle bracelets at me.

"But Val, can't you see? I *love* accessories!"

Awesome. My partners in crime are an ancient, air-headed cabaret dancer in high heels and a Hell's Angels wannabe that couldn't run thirty feet without going into cardiac arrest.

My confidence dropped down a mine shaft.

I should just call the whole thing off, before we end up sharing a cell in Sing Sing....

"Are you two *sure* you want to do this thing?" I asked.

"Absolutely, sarge," Double H said, and saluted me in his cop shirt and cap.

"You're darn tootin'!" Laverne answered brightly, and shot me two thumbs up.

I sighed and resigned myself to my fate.

"Okay, then. It's on. Laverne, you ride with me. Double H, you follow behind, like you're a motorcycle cop."

"Ten-four, good buddy," Double H said, causing the doubt that had crept into my brain to compound exponentially.

THE SLEAZY STRIP CENTER was deserted. I guess attorneys, hookers and sexual deviants liked to sleep in.

"Here we go," Double H said, and turned the knob on Finkerman's office door. The fat, fake cop had picked the lock in under thirty seconds, and employed even fewer swear words in the process.

So far, so good.

The door gave way to his safe-cracker charms, and we piled into Finkerman's office like it was Black Friday at Walmart.

"Look around for the video tapes," I said. "Laverne, you check out Fargo's desk here."

"Is that Fargo?" Laverne asked, and picked up a framed photo of the two nearly identical men standing side by side.

"Yeah."

Double H whistled. "No doubt those two are from the same gene pool."

"Gene pool?" I said. "More like scum pond. Double H, I think there's a storage closet down the hall. Finkerman keeps a box of...uh...*stuff* in there. That may be where he stashes the tapes, too. You take the closet. I'll check his private office."

"Ten four," Double H said, and waddled down the hallway.

I was almost through pilfering through the papers on Finkerman's desk when Double H came in toting a box of VCR tapes.

"You were right," he said, and handed me a tape. "This one's marked this week."

I grabbed the tape and stuck it in an old VCR on Finkerman's desk. I found a remote control and clicked the sticky "on" button. The TV monitor mounted on the wall buzzed to life. I mashed a button on the VCR and the tape began to roll. So did a parade of call girls.

"That's *some* clientele he's got," Double H said.

I shook my head at the stream of hookers that came and went out of Finkerman's office, teasing the bejeebers out of Fargo as they left. It was like watching *The Making of a Young Scumbag* on PBS.

"This tape is from the camera mounted by the front door," I said. "We need the tape from Finkerman's office camera."

"Roger that." Double H said, and began pawing through the tapes in the box.

I was about to stop the hooker parade tape when a mousy-looking woman came on screen.

I recognized her face.

"Here's the latest names from the overdue book list," the woman said, and handed Fargo a slip of paper. "Thirty-seven names," she said, and pushed a pair of librarian glasses up on her nose. "That's thirty-seven bucks you owe me."

Oh my gosh! Victoria really was a librarian!

"Right," Fargo said, and took a box from a locked drawer in his desk. He opened the petty cash box and counted out thirty-seven ones.

Victoria, the library-faced lady from my writer's class, snatched the cash and shot Fargo an evil grin.

"Nice doing business with you."

Fargo smiled weakly. Victoria left. As the door closed behind her, Fargo put a finger gun to his temple and pulled the thumb trigger.

Double H and I exchanged glances.

"I *know* her!" I said, and pulled out the tape. "Okay. So, we've got the source of Finkerman's mailing list. Now we just need to get Finkerman on tape admitting to extortion."

"Try this one," Double H said, and handed me a tape. I stuck it in the VCR and got a close up look at a body part I never knew existed.

"Ugh!" I groaned and covered my eyes. "Double H, you take control. Fast forward until you see a woman in a short jean skirt wrestling with Finkerman on his desk.

"Whatever you say, boss."

After three false alarms, Double H hit pay dirt.

"Here's another one," he said.

I cracked opened an eye for a look. There I was, wriggling around on the desk with Finkerman. Like all the other images on the tape, I wish I'd never seen it. I had enough cellulite on the back of my thighs to start my own fat farm.

"That's the tape," I said.

I shut off the VCR, grabbed the tape out of it, and crammed it into my purse with the other one.

"Okay, Double H, let's get out of here."

My partner in crime nodded, and we headed toward the exit. Down the hallway, we heard someone knocking around in the storeroom. The aroma of brewing coffee permeated the air.

Oh, crap!

"Finkerman's here," I whispered.

"Wait here," Double H said, and crept toward the storeroom door.

Too nervous to sit still, I followed the portly fake policeman down the hall. Double H put a paw on the doorknob to the storeroom and jerked it open. I gasped as he raised his meaty fist like a club. Suddenly, he cocked his head sideways and let his arm fall to his side.

I peeked into the storeroom. There, by the coffee machine, stood the ancient remains of the Bond girl in *Goldfinger*. Making coffee.

"Laverne!" I yelled, causing Double H to fart.

"Don't scare me like that!" he said. "I thought I told you to wait over there!"

"What are you doing in there?" I asked Laverne.

"Making coffee," she said, and beamed the full range of her dentures at me. "I thought you two might could use something to drink."

"We found the tapes," I said. "Turn off the machine. We need to get out of here."

Laverne mashed the "off" button with a shiny red nail tip and tottered over toward us.

"We're the three banditos!" she chirped.

"Right," I said. "Now let's get outta here before we get caught."

Laverne and I trailed behind Double H like ducklings. But just as he reached a huge paw for the front door, the tarnished brass knob began to turn on its own.

Oh, geeze. Crap on a cracked up cracker.

Chapter Thirty-Seven

"Someone's at the door!" Laverne squealed, making me wish I had a roll of duct tape in my purse along with the rolls of quarters.

I grabbed her by the arm and Double H shoved us down the hallway out of sight.

Over Double H's labored breathing, I could hear the door squeak open, then slam closed.

Ferrol Finkerman grumbled, "I told that dolt a hundred times to lock that blasted door."

"Wait here," Double H whispered to us, then, before I could stop him, the pretend policeman stepped out of the hallway and into the room.

"Hold it right there," he said to Finkerman.

Finkerman's voice was an octave higher when he said, "Look, buddy. I told your boss I'd have his money *tomorrow*."

"Well, tomorrow came early," Double H said. "Have a seat."

Laverne and I huddled together in the hallway like orphans in a storm. I heard the familiar sound of duct tape ripping off a roll. Laverne opened her mouth. I put my hand over it.

"Is that really necessary?" Finkerman asked. His voice sounded more annoyed that fearful. "Look, I've got fifty bucks in my wallet. Can't we work something out, just between you and me?"

"It's not *money* we want," Double H said.

"*We*? You mean you're not here for...*you know who?*"

"Not likely. You can come out now, ladies," Double H announced.

I took a tentative peek around the corner. Finkerman was straddling Fargo's chair. His ankles were duct taped to the front legs of it. His wrists appeared to be bound together behind the chair's backrest.

"Fremden!" he called out.

Finkerman's voice sounded nearly giddy with relief. Then it switched back to his normal snarky, nasal whine.

"Well, well," he said, looking at me with something resembling admiration. "I didn't think you had it in you."

"There's a lot *you* don't know about me," I said, trying to sound tough. But my guts were seesawing between Southern belle guilt and Valiant Stranger's desire for justice.

Crap on a cracker.

I hadn't planned on stringing up Finkerman. But then again, I finally had the jerk right where I wanted him. Why waste the opportunity?

I swaggered up to the hog-tied lawyer, my heart beating in my throat.

"I know *everything* about you, Finkerman," I lied with as much bravado as I could muster, considering there was a gold-lame clad septuagenarian by my side rooting me on like a proud grandma.

"You do, huh?" Finkerman sneered. "Like *what?*"

"I know you're in cahoots with Victoria from the public library. She's *married*, you know," I said, winging it. "Her husband might not take the news of your affair too well. I hear he's a retired football player. Tight end, I believe."

Finkerman shrugged. "So?"

"Drop your suit against me, Finkerman, and you won't end up with a football shoved up your end zone."

Finkerman laughed. "*That's* all you've got on me?"

I bit my lip and looked over at Double H. I kind of didn't want to go where I was going next. But I kind of *did*, too....

"Not exactly," I said. "See this fine, upstanding police officer here? He's investigating a series of break-ins in the area. Laverne and I are...uh...*aiding* his investigation."

Finkerman rolled his eyes. "What a crock of bull."

"Maybe, maybe not," I said. "But let me remind you, Finkerman, there's nobody here to plead your case – except a shyster scumbag attorney. And he's kind of tied up at the moment."

Double H snorted. Laverne cocked her head at me, confused. Finkerman blew out a breath.

"Give it up, Fremden. Nothing short of five grand is gonna get you off the hook with me."

"No? We'll see about that."

I turned to Double H. "Go ahead, officer. Commence operation *Follicle Failure*."

Double H reached over and plucked a frizzy hair from Finkerman's head. The attorney's shifty eyes grew as big as boiled eggs.

"What are you doing?" he hissed.

"Collecting a DNA sample to compare against that of the perpetrator burgling nearby businesses," I said.

"Har har," Finkerman spat. "You've had your fun, Fremden. Now let me go!"

"I'm afraid I'm gonna need another sample," Double H said, and plucked another hair from Finkerman's thin, balding pate. He studied the end. "Darn. Again, no follicle."

Finkerman's sneer lost its edge. "You've got to be joking."

"'Fraid not," Double H said. "You know, the DNA thingy down at the lab is kinda unreliable. I might need two, three, or maybe a couple hundred hairs, just to be on the safe side."

Finkerman's face turned the color of a pastor's posterior.

"You wouldn't," he whispered.

Harvey plucked another hair. Finkerman lost his swagger – along with a follicle.

"Stop!" Finkerman screeched. "All right already! Two grand and I drop the suit!"

Double H looked at me.

I shook my head. "No deal."

Double H reached over to pull another frizzy hair. Finkerman scrunched his neck down like a turtle trying to duck into its shell. Considering the painful expression on his face, we might as well have been pulling his *teeth*.

"Hold up a moment," I said to Double H. I reached in my purse, fished a small tape recorder out and hit "record."

I looked into Finkerman's bulging eyes. "This is your last chance, Finkerman. For the record, did you try to extort money from Laverne Cowens over an overdue library book?"

Finkerman shot an angry glance over at Laverne.

"I don't recall such a thing."

"Finkerman, your memory's as convenient as your morals," I said. "Go ahead, officer. Obtain another sample."

I nodded at Double H and he relieved Finkerman of another kinky, reddish-brown head hair.

Finkerman whined like an abandoned puppy. "Okay! Okay! I admit it. Are you satisfied?"

"Not quite," I said. "Now, tell me that your suit against me is baseless, and therefore you're formally dropping it."

Finkerman pursed his thin lips. "Two hundred bucks and we're even?"

"Some folks never learn," Double H tutted and shook his head.

Finkerman squirmed as Double H reached up and removed his police cap, then his do-rag. The biker's pale, naked dome shone in the fluorescent lighting like an albino bowling ball.

Double H leaned over until the top of his shiny head was six inches from Finkerman's pointy nose.

"Take a good look at your future, scumbag," Double H huffed.

Finkerman's expression couldn't have been more horrified if he'd have been looking at himself in his own coffin.

Double H straightened to standing. "Gimme your cellphone," he said to Finkerman. "I'll have one of my lovely assistants here put *Hair Club for Men* on your speed-dial."

Finkerman groaned like a certain figurine that had recently met its demise under my Hammer of Justice.

Double H laughed and slapped his do-rag back over his glowing-white, billiard ball of a noggin.

"Do yourself a favor, buddy," Double H said. "Stop pestering these two fine ladies here. Just agree to the terms stated, and we'll disappear...*before* the rest of your hair does."

Finkerman whined, and nodded his semi-bald head.

Chapter Thirty-Eight

I high-stepped it out of Finkerman's office and did a victory dance in the parking lot.

"Wahooo! We *did* it!" I yelled, "And we've got it all on tape!"

"Woo hoo!" Laverne hooted and kicked up her gold high heels. "We got him all on the duct tape! Val, you're a genius!"

Well, that makes one of us....

I grinned and hooked arms with the golden Vegas showgirl, and we spun around in the parking lot like the world's most unbalanced atomic element.

Double H laughed and clapped out a beat with his beefy hands until I got dizzy and stopped the show. I was so giddy with relief that I hugged them both.

"What do we owe you?" I asked Double H as I unwrapped my arms from around his big belly.

Double H grinned and shook his head. "I don't want your money, girls. To tell the truth, that was the most fun I've had in ages. In fact, I'd *pay you* money if I could go back inside and finish off that twerp's frizzy fro."

The thought of Finkerman looking as bald as Squidward from *Spongebob Squarepants* sent me into a giggle fit. But it also made my heart tingle with guilt. Southern pride was a weird thing, indeed.

I tried to justify my actions to myself.

What was done needed to be done. And besides, what was done, well, was already done.

"Here's your cop shirt back," Double H said, peeling it from his ample torso.

The tattered blue shirt was limp with sweat. Both sleeves were torn at the armpits, and a couple of buttonholes were, shall I say, *enlarged.* Tom's shirt was beyond repair. But that was a problem for another day. Today, we would focus on *victory!*

"So, how about a celebratory lunch?" I asked. "It's on me!"

"I'd love to," Double H said, "but no can do. I've got another assignment across town."

"Well, it was great to meet you," I said. "And thanks again for your help."

"Likewise. If you ever need me again, here's my card."

Double H handed me a black card. The only thing on it were the letters HH and a phone number...in red.

"Will do," I said, as he hauled a beefy leg over the seat of his Harley.

He turned a key in the ignition and the shiny, chrome ape-hanger roared to life. I felt Laverne's arm slip around my waist, and we watched Double H disappear out of sight, like Santa Claus in the throes of a full-blown, mid-life crisis.

"Well, looks like it's you and me, kid," Laverne said in a voice like Humphrey Bogart with laryngitis.

I laughed. "What's say you and me split this joint?"

"Suits me fine."

I motioned toward Maggie. "Your chariot awaits, Madame."

Laverne giggled like a schoolgirl and let go of my waist. She moved a foot toward the car, stepped in a pothole and nearly toppled over in her heels.

I shook my head. "Laverne, why do you *always* wear high heels?"

Laverne looked down at her shoes as if she'd never seen them before, then looked up at me and shrugged.

"Habit, I guess, honey. In Vegas, they always told us showgirls that a gal's just one pair of Birkenstocks away from the slippery slope to Slobsville."

My ears burned. Not *only* was I wearing Birkenstocks – I had on sweatpants, a ratty t-shirt, no makeup, and my hair was in a ponytail greasy enough to fry eggs.

I wasn't just a *citizen* of Slobsville...I was their village idiot.

"Oh," I said, and held open the passenger door for Laverne and her glitzy gold outfit. "Compared to you, Laverne, I guess I look like a frump-a-dump."

Laverne eyed me up and down, shrugged her shoulders and gave me a pursed-lip smile.

"I dunno about that, honey."

"I'm right, aren't I?" I asked. "I don't get it. How do you keep yourself so...together?"

Laverne smiled. "I learned a long time ago that life ain't a poker game, honey."

"What do you mean?"

"When it comes to outward appearances, you don't hold your best cards for last, Val. You play *them* first. You don't show a fella the crummy stuff until later. You know...after you've lulled him into complacency."

"Oh."

Laverne slid her scrawny butt into the seat. "Thanks for offering to buy lunch, honey, but I'm gonna pass."

"Why?"

"A girl's gotta watch her figure. And I plan on eating like a pig at the party tonight."

Holy crap! Winky and Winnie's engagement party! I'd forgotten all about it...again!

"Uh...okay. No problem Laverne."

I climbed in the car and turned the ignition key. Maggie rumbled to life, and I peeled out of the parking lot of Finkerman's office. As I tooled toward home listening to Laverne belting out, *I Did It My Way*, I realized I was envious of her in many ways.

Laverne knew herself, and actually *liked* who she was. So much so, she refused to change for anyone – not even J.D. And what's more, she afforded everyone around her the same privilege. She was a real-life, living example of that old saying, "Why don't you be you and I'll be me."

I glanced over and smiled at Laverne. She returned the favor. I knew deep in my heart that the old woman loved me just the way I was. And, I guess, in my own slightly more judgmental way, I loved her the way she was, too.

"What'd you get Winky and Winnie?" Laverne asked when she'd finished the first chorus of her song.

I nearly hit the brakes. Not only had I forgotten about the party – I'd forgotten to get the trailer twins an engagement gift, too.

"It's a surprise," I said. "How about you?"

Laverne winked. "The same," she said, and began belting out another verse of *I Did It My Way*.

I drummed my nails on the steering wheel in time to Laverne's off-beat serenade, and racked my brain for an appropriate gift for Winnie and Winky. But I came up blank.

What could I get a pair of rednecks who were no longer in need of a pot to piss in?

Chapter Thirty-Nine

Maggie rumbled into my driveway. I shifted into park and cut the ignition. Two missions had been accomplished. Finkerman had been vanquished, and I had my gift for Winnie and Winky.

In the seat next to me was a gift bag containing a hundred-dollar gift certificate to the Dollar Store.

I waved to Laverne. I'd dropped her off in front of her house, and she was toddling her way toward her front door, toting a Dollar Store bag nearly big enough to use as a pup tent.

Laverne hadn't needed any arm twisting to make a stop on the way home from our victorious gig of relieving Finkerman of his follicles. In fact, it had been her idea. She'd taken a coupon from her purse and waved it at me, informing me that the Dollar Store was having a two-for one sale on her favorite Skinny Dip dinners. Apparently, the new foil-pouch version didn't need refrigerating – and it didn't go over well in test markets, either.

I went inside, plopped the gift bag on the kitchen counter and frowned. Somehow, a generic gift card seemed too impersonal for such an auspicious occasion. I pondered the thought for a moment, then realized I was in possession of something I knew the two trailer tots would love. I went and got it and added it to the gift bag.

According to the clock on the kitchen wall, it was approaching two o'clock, and I was still in black sweats, t-shirt and Birkenstocks.

I looked like a cat burglar who'd just robbed Woodstock.

I wanted to take a tip from Laverne and make myself attractive before Tom played his hand and left me at the ugly table. But one look at my reflection in the bathroom mirror told me my makeover would require more time and money than I had to invest at present. What I really needed was a facelift, a tummy tuck, and a month at a fat farm.

But seeing as how I only had three hours and thirty-seven minutes, and closet full of clothes so outdated even the Salvation Army wouldn't even take them, I had to work with what I had.

I rifled through my closet, thinking about who would be at the party tonight. Winnie and Winky didn't need impressing. Neither did Cold Cuts or Bill. Milly and Vance already knew not to expect much. And I'd already had a couple of years to lower Tom's expectations....

But then I thought about Jorge and his glamorous new girlfriend Sherryl. Tom was once married to her cousin, Darryl.

Darryl!

The thought of Tom's ex-wife sent a wave of insecurity crashing down on me.

Darryl was gorgeous, elegant, mild-tempered.... In other words, everything *I wasn't.* Compared to Darryl's sexy Spanish fly, I was a redneck cockroach. And a slob. And now... a petty criminal!

I was a walking disaster!

I rifled through my closet again, Laverne's words echoing in my head. Maybe it was time to give those impossible high heels I'd been saving a spin...

I grabbed the shoebox out of the closet and crammed my feet into the six-inch, silver-sequined heels. Two steps later, the balls of my feet might as well have been treading on stingray spines.

I wish someone could take fat out of my stomach and put it in the bottom of my feet....

I winced in pain and looked up at myself in the vanity mirror. The grimace on my face made me looked like Doo-Doo Daddy – in a brown, greasy wig.

Ugh!

It was too late. I'd already slipped down the slope to Slobsville. If high heels and Epiladys were any indicator, beauty required pain. Was it my fault I had a low tolerance for it?

When was the last time I felt glamorous?

I strained my brain. It had been a few years ago. Laverne had helped me glitz up for Tom's policeman's ball. Even though that night had ended in a disaster, it had started well. And maybe this time would be different.

I kicked off the killer shoes and padded into the kitchen for a gin and tonic. I downed it, then dialed Laverne's number.

I WAS STANDING IN THE tub, wearing nothing but a G-string and a worried expression.

"Trust me," Laverne said, and popped the lid off a can of Fake 'n' Bake, a self-tanning foam she'd picked up at the Dollar Store.

She squirted a load of foam into her hands and began to rub me down like an ancient masseuse with inch-long red fingernails.

"When I'm done with you, Tom won't know what hit him," she said. "This is my number one glamour trick, honey!"

I fought against the rising tide of doubt gnawing at my gut, and took a long chug of the gin and tonic in my hand.

"OPEN YOUR EYES, HONEY!"

I did as Laverne commanded. The first thing I saw in the mirror was her horsey smile and beaming double row of dentures.

The second thing I saw was the orange-skinned transvestite standing next to her.

I stared, speechless and transfixed.

Laverne had transformed every inch of me, from my teased-up hair to my clowned-up face. My fake, press-on nails matched perfectly with the painted-on gold-lame cat suit she'd squeezed me into.

True to her word, Laverne had kept her promise. Tom really wouldn't know what hit him. And I was in desperate need of hitting something myself.

I could have possibly coped if I could have gotten ahold of a chocolate fix. But someone had stolen my stash of that, too. It was as if the world was conspiring against me to make me crazy. I looked in the mirror again and conceded defeat.

Chapter Forty

Okay. This was no longer just a hobby...it was bordering on mental illness.

I looked down at the rough, chipped-off stump where Pizza Man's hand used to be. I wanted to add to his missing body parts.

My fingers itched and curled a little tighter around the handle of my new Hammer of Justice. Despite its gleaming, stainless-steel head, the hammer's shine paled in comparison to my glittery gold fingernails and the matching cat-suit my butt was crammed into.

I blew a strand of teased hair out of my eyes.

Does it still count if I'm unrecognizable?

My conscience kicked in for a microsecond.

Val! Get a grip! What's wrong *with you?*

I should've been celebrating my good fortune. My troubles with Finkerman were in the past. I was in sole possession of the embarrassing VHS tape of me scrounging through a box of sex toys wearing sparkly hot-pants. And in a few minutes, I'd be leaving to go to a party to celebrate the upcoming nuptials of some good friends.

But instead of feeling joyful, I felt like a freak.

And looked the part, too.

I'd wanted to knock Tom's socks off tonight. But thanks to Laverne's ridiculous makeover, I was worried I might be mistaken for a space alien from a low-budget sci-fi movie. I couldn't leave my house

189

looking like this, and there was no time to return to my home planet before Tom got home....

So I'd done the only thing I could think to do. I'd drunk another gin and tonic. My fourth. That's when I'd gotten the idea to waste Pizza Man.

I was tipsy and angry and ready to punch someone's lights out.

This was all Tom's fault! If he hadn't gone and sold that dreamcatcher, none of this would have happened!

I hiccoughed.

Well, at least some of it *wouldn't have happened.*

I snatched the Pizza Man amputee off the kitchen counter and eyed the sliding glass door. It lead to the backyard, and the concrete execution block where my Hammer of Justice did its dirty work.

If I opened that door, there would be no turning back.

I took a wobbly, tentative step toward the back door. All of a sudden, like a scene from a TV detective show, the front door flew open. A cop rushed in and drew his pistol on me.

I gasped, and dropped both the hammer and the figurine. Pizza Man shattered on impact, and scattered his little Italian remains all over the terrazzo floor.

"Who are you?" the cop asked. "What are you doing here?"

According to my inebriated mind, I had two choices. One, I could fess up to my crime. Or two, I could clam up and let Tom haul the crazy cat woman off to jail, none the wiser it was me.

I debated for a moment, but before I could decide my fate, I broke down into tears instead.

"YOU DESERVE APPLE PIE," I sobbed as I hung over Tom's shoulder like a limp dishrag. "I'm nothing but mincemeat."

I hiccoughed and sniffed and blew my nose on Tom's cop shirt.

"What are you talking about, Val?" Tom asked as he hauled me to the couch and sat me down.

"Darryl," I wailed. "If *she* wasn't enough for you, *I'll* never be."

Tom sat beside me, took me gently by the shoulders, and looked me in the eyes.

"So *this* is what this is all about?"

"Look at me!" I said.

Tom stifled a grin. "I'm trying to, but I can't make out anything that's recognizable."

"I'm hideous," I whimpered, and broke out in a fresh round of tears.

"Oh, Val. Come on!"

"Why don't you just *hic* go back to *her*," I sobbed. "She seems like a...like a really pretty *hic* pretty nice person."

"Geeze, Val. Darryl *is* a nice person. That wasn't the problem."

"What was?" I asked, not sure I wanted to know the answer.

"Darryl and I...we didn't make it because we didn't want the same things, Val. Not because of the way she looked or how she acted."

Tom hugged me to his chest. I took the opportunity to add to the mural of makeup smears I'd already applied to his shirt.

"Tell me, Val," Tom whispered softly. "What do *you* want?"

"From you?" I asked.

"From *life*."

"To be happy," I said, then sniffed.

Tom lifted my sagging head with a gentle tug on my chin.

"Me, too." He sighed. "So, I guess that settles it."

Suddenly half sober, I stared into Tom's sea-green eyes.

"What do you mean?" I asked.

Tom smiled and shook his head.

"Silly girl. It means I'm sticking with you."

My heart pinged. "Really?"

"Really."

Tom lifted my chin and kissed me.

I smiled. "Thanks."

Tom laughed, looked down at the floor, then back up at me.

"I also think it means I win our wager, Val. My chair stays."

I jerked my chin out of his hand. "What? Why?"

"Admit it. I caught you red-handed, Val. A hammer in one hand, a figurine in the other."

"But I didn't smash it!"

"Right."

"I dropped it! You saw it yourself. It's not the same thing!"

"But you were *going* to. The hammer proves intent."

"No! I wasn't!"

"No? Then why'd you have the hammer?"

"Uh...I was going to nail something."

Tom shook his head and grinned.

"Worst alibi ever. But okay. I'll buy it for now. Our wager's still on."

"Good." I bit my lip, sniffed, and wiped my eye with my hand. My fingers came back purple and black. I groaned inside.

My face must look like a finger painting done by a two-year old.

"So tell me, what's with the getup?" Tom asked. "Winky's party? It isn't redneck-formal, is it?"

"Ha ha," I said.

Tom looked me up and down and shook his head.

"Okay. You got me, Val. Why the cat-suit and heels?"

I shrugged. "I dunno. It's just...well, I didn't want to look like a slob, okay?"

"Well, now you've turned *me* into a slob."

"Sorry about your shirt," I said, and wiped it with my hand. My efforts only made the lipstick and mascara smears even worse.

Tom took my hand. "That's not what I'm talking about."

"No? What *are* you talking about, then?"

Tom wagged his eyebrows at me seductively. "Can't you see I'm *slob*bering?"

I barked out an unexpected laugh.

"Now *there's* the old bad-joke Tom I know and love."

"You *love* me," Tom said dreamily, and jokingly put a hand to his heart.

"Unfortunately, yes," I said, and punched his upper arm. "Now be a love and help crazy cat lady get out of this getup."

I reached down and started to take off my killer heels.

Tom stopped me.

"Wait," he said. "Allow me."

As Tom unbuckled the clasp on my exquisite but ridiculously painful high heels, a voice piped up in my tipsy brain and reminded me that I was supposed to be mad at him. Tom *had* sold Goober's dreamcatcher, after all.

I froze in place, and, for a split second, considered rebuffing Tom's help.

Then another voice whispered in my ear and reminded me of something more important.

What are you winning, kiddo, holding onto your anger?

The answer was as clear as my gin and tonic.

Nothing, Glad. Not a dad-blame thing.

Chapter Forty-One

For late July, it turned out to be a surprisingly nice evening. There was a respectable breeze off the Gulf, and the humidity was under ninety percent, making it perfect for top-down cruising. And, after passing Tom's sobriety test, he'd okayed me to drive.

Earlier that evening, Tom's princely performance had proven to me that I didn't have to be a glamor girl to earn his love. I only had to want to be happy – and have a skin hue within the range of the species known as Homo sapiens.

After undoing my shoes, Tom had helped me remove most of the traces of my attempt at glamour trannydom. Instead of Day-Glo orange, my skin was now glowing pink from a good scrubbing.

I'd also removed the fake fingernails and replaced the gold cat-suit and killer heels with Tom's favorite sundress and a pair of cute, sensible sandals. I felt as fresh as a daisy could in the mid-summer heat.

"So, are you excited about the party?" I asked Tom, and mashed the gas pedal. Maggie rumbled and rattled her way down US 19, toward the Redneck Riviera known as Pinellas Park.

"To be honest, I'm more excited about picking up the puppy tomorrow," Tom said. "Speaking of which, isn't it time we finally decided on a name, Val? I don't want the poor pup to be confused any more than he has to be."

I glanced over at Tom. His blond bangs were blowing in the breeze. The fading sunset had turned them strawberry gold.

"Like I told you, Tom. You can name him *anything* but Sir Albert Snoggles, III."

"Then Zalamanchicolista it is."

My nose crinkled. "Huh?"

"You said *anything*."

"I meant anything within the realm of human reason...and *pronunciation*."

"There you go again," Tom laughed. "Rewriting the rules as you go along."

My eyes narrowed in mock outrage. "What are you talking about? I *never* do that."

Tom snorted. "Hornswaggle."

I took another glance over at Tom, uncertain if his last comment was aimed at *me* or the puppy.

"Whoa! Take a right here," he said, and jabbed a finger at a fast-approaching road sign.

"I know," I said, even though I knew darn well I'd have driven right past the street if Tom hadn't said anything.

I jerked Maggie's steering wheel to the right and performed a hairpin turn.

"See?" I said, as I maneuvered safely onto the side road. "I *told* you I had it under control."

Tom shifted his eyes from me back to the road. He blew out a breath and said, "Jabbermutt."

AS WE PULLED UP TO Winky and Winnie's new double-wide trailer, Tom and I couldn't help but notice the long, black hearse parked in front. A big, red bow was fastened to its hood, and a *You-Haul-It* trailer was hitched to the hearse's back end.

"I was wrong," Tom said. "I guess you *can* take it with you."

We looked at each other and laughed.

"Let the weirdness begin," I said, and opened the car door. As I slammed it behind me, my cellphone rang.

"It's Cold Cuts," I said. "I should take this."

"Okay," Tom said. "I'll see you inside."

As Tom made his way through the jumble of cars parked outside, I clicked the green button on my cellphone.

"Hey! What's up?"

"Bad news," Cold Cuts said. "I'm sorry, but Bill and I can't make it tonight. Could you tell Winnie and Winky we're sorry?"

"Uh. Sure. What's happened?"

"Nothing, really. Our sitter for Bill's dad crapped out on us."

"Why don't you just bring Freddie along?"

"He's too unpredictable, Val, with the dementia and all."

"How bad can he be?"

"Well, tonight he put his socks in his soup, and his pants on his – oh no!"

"What's happened?"

"Listen, Val. I've got to go. Freddie just ran out the door wearing my high heels."

"If he's like me, he can't get too far in them."

"Right. But, unfortunately, that was *all* he was wearing. Geeze, Val! Half the guests around here must think we're running a nudist resort."

"Sorry about that."

"It's okay. At least he's happy. That's what matters."

"You're *so* right about that, Cold Cuts. It's a shame you can't make it. You'll be missed."

"I miss you guys, too. Give everyone my love, okay?"

"I will."

"Thanks. I – Oh, geeze! Freddie! Sorry, Val I've got to go."

The line went dead.

I sighed, stuck my phone in my purse, and counted my blessings. Then I made my way through the parked cars toward another place full of people slightly off their rockers...and all the more loveable for it.

Chapter Forty-Two

"Howdy, Val pal!" Winky hollered as I walked inside his double-wide trailer. Dressed in a black Stetson, an oversized dress shirt and fancy Western jeans, he looked like the maître de at a roadside rodeo.

"Come on in and get you some champagne and caviar," he said, and handed me a clear, plastic cup full of bubbly, pale-yellow liquid.

"Well! Isn't this all fancy!" I said.

"Yep. I seen it on that show, *Lifestyles of the Rich and Famous*. Here, try one a these horse ovary things."

Winky daintily picked up a tray full of crackers topped with grey goop and shoved it at me.

"What is it?" I asked.

"Balooger caviar," Winky said proudly. "Between you and me, it was mighty 'spensive. But hey. Nothin's too good for my Winnie."

"Huh."

I picked up a cracker off the tray and sniffed it. Winky leaned in and whispered in my ear.

"I know it don't look like much, Val. But when that balooger stuff come, it wat'n even cooked. I throwed it in the skillet with some bacon grease and mashed it up with some smoked mullet spread. What a ya thank?"

I took a bite. Against all odds, it was freaking delicious.

"Wow! That's fabulous, Winky!"

He beamed. "You know what they say, Val. Bacon can solve purty near every problem known to mankind."

I laughed and raised an eyebrow. "Even Laverne's cooking?"

Winky's features scrunched together in the center of his face.

"Well, it ain't *that* miraculous. I do believe that woman put the devil in devilled eggs."

I stifled a laugh. "Sshh! There she is."

Panic shot through Winky's face. "Quick, Val! Tell me. What'd she bring?"

"I don't know," I whispered. "She rode over with J.D."

"Dang it," Winky sulked. Suddenly, his face brightened. "I know. I'll get my private eye on it."

My eyebrows collided. "What? You have a private investigator?"

"Yep. Hired him on account a whoever keeps callin' code enforcement on us down at the donut shop."

"Wouldn't it be easer just to comply with the codes, Winky?"

"Maybe. But this here's *personal*. And there ain't no way to legislate against somebody bein' a jerk."

"That's for sure," I commiserated. "Lord knows, I wish there was. What's the complaint?"

"Same thang as always," Winky said. "Loiterin'. Get's so a feller can't even serve the public."

"What do you mean, 'serve the public'?"

"Well, ever since I started Bum-a-Bite Fridays and Spare-a-Spill Saturdays, somebody's gone and got all riled up."

"What on earth are you talking about?"

"You know, Val. Like Winnie done fer me at Davie's Donuts. After two o'clock, I give out all the leftover donut pieces and undrunk coffee to the hungry fellers hangin' around. I'm payin' it forward. See?"

Unfortunately, I could.

"And nobody cares about it being a health hazard?" I asked.

"Huh? Naw. Only complaint I got so far was them fellers some-times takes a nap afterward...you know, in the sand dunes and whatnot around the shop."

"You don't say."

I reached for another cracker and popped it into my mouth. I'd never had beluga caviar before, and probably never would again. My cheeks were crammed full when Winnie came up to join us.

"Val!" she squealed. "Did you see what Winky got me? My very own You Haul It! Now we all can go yard-salin' whenever we want!"

"I've never seen anything like it," I said. "It's truly one of a kind."

I hope.

Winky blushed with redneck pride.

"But I'm curious," I said. "Why a *hearse?*"

"Oh," Winky chimed in. "On account a my cousin Tater had it layin' around in his shop. He was gonna make it into a hot rod, but changed his mind. He'd already put a diesel V-8 engine in it. Said it'd be great for haulin' a trailer. And it's already extra roomy in the back and all. Purty smart, huh?"

"Makes perfect sense," I said.

"And economicable," Winky said.

"How do you figure that?" I asked.

"Val, ever'body knows deiseline's a whole lot cheaper'n gas."

"Oh. Sure," I said. "Well, at any rate, congratulations on your up-coming wedding. I have to say, I honestly can't think of another couple who belong together as much as you two do."

"Can you believe it?" Winky asked, and wrapped an arm around Winnie's waist. "In a couple a months, this little lady's gonna be the wind beneath my wings."

"And let me guess, Winky," I said. "You'll be the wind beneath her *sheets.*"

Winnie burst out laughing. It took Winky another second, then his woodpecker staccato joined in.

"Oh. Here's your gift," I said as I wiped tears of laughter from my eyes.

"You didn't have to go and do that!" Winky said. But before I could reply he grabbed the gift bag from my hand, dug through it and ripped into the envelope inside.

"Woo hoo! Looky here, Winnie! A hunnert dollars for the Dollar Store! Geeze, Val! We can get us like, a whole bunch a stuff with this!"

"That's the idea," I said. I grinned and turned to Winnie. "There's one more thing inside."

Winnie grabbed the bag from Winkie and pulled out the remaining gift.

"Well isn't that the cutest thing ever!" she said. She pushed her red glasses up on her nose to study the figurine. "It says here, 'Gee your affable.'"

"Giraffe...able," I said lamely.

A familiar arm wrapped around my waist. Tom had come over to join us. "A figurine?" he whispered in my ear, and tugged playfully at my waist. "How original."

"How cute is that, honey?" Winnie said.

She handed Winky the long-necked, bottom-heavy figurine and wrapped me in a bear hug, breaking Tom's hold on my waist.

"Val, you still got that Dr. Dingbat feller?" Winky asked.

"Uh...I don't know what you're talking about," I said, and shook my head ever so slightly. I should have known my effort at discretion would be futile when it came to Winky.

"You know," he said. "That there statue of that there guy on the toilet. The one you brought by the shop the other day, right a'fore you showed up in hot-pants and went to dumpster divin'. Woo hoo! Was that ever a sight!"

Winky turned to Winnie and Tom, his head cocked and one eyebrow raised.

"What?" Tom asked.

"You should a been there, Tommy boy!" Winky continued. "You may not know it, but our gal Val here's got an original Dr. Dingbat. That there Difficult Defecation figure's worth twenty grand."

Tom gave me some side eye and asked, "Why were you dumpster diving?"

"On a'cause a Val went and threw the battery away," Winky answered for me. "You should a seen her, Tom. When she was done, she looked like a skunk that'd been dragged through a knothole back'ards. Come to think of it, she smelled like one, too."

I couldn't decide whether to laugh along with Winky's deranged cackle or spit a fireball at him. I mostly just wanted to melt into a crack in the floor.

"As I recall," I said, "it was *you* who threw the battery away, Winky."

Winky shrugged. "Well, if you wanner get *picky* about it."

"What are you doing with all these figurines, Val?" Tom asked. "And how on earth could one be worth that much money?"

"It isn't. At least, not without the battery," I said, and shot a dirty look at Winky.

"It was part of a series," Winky said, oblivious. "Developed by some fancy doctor type who wishes to remain autonomous."

"Anonymous," I corrected. "I can't imagine why."

"Me neither," Winky said. "I seen a picture of the whole Dr. Dingbat line on the internet. Let's see. There was Gangrenous Gout. Flaming Flatulence. The Perpetual Pooper. My personal favorite, Bodacious Butt Boil –."

"Thanks. We get the picture," I said.

Tom turned and studied me. "So where is this twenty-grand figurine now?"

I grabbed another cracker from the tray. "Have you tried these? They're delicious."

Tom stared me down. "Val –"

"Heeelppp!"

For a second, I wondered if the tiny voice inside my head had grown vocal chords.

"Help me!" the voice called out again.

Tom's head cocked to one side. "It's coming from outside!"

"Shore is!" Winky agreed.

We all stepped over to the front door. Winky jerked it open.

I peered outside, and for once in my adult life, I believed in Christmas miracles – even in July.

Chapter Forty-Three

On the lawn in front of Winky's trailer, a disheveled Santa and a disgruntled elf were brawling it out like a couple of drunken hobos.

Santa had the elf in a headlock. The little guy reached up and jerked the fat man's red do-rag over his eyes. Temporarily blinded, Santa let go and pulled the rag from his face.

"Double H!" Winky and I cried out.

I shot Winky an incredulous look. "You *know* him?"

Tom shot me an incredulous look. "*You* know him?"

"That there feller's my private eye," Winky said. "We gots to do somethin' afore J.D. and him does 'emselves in!"

Tom's face shifted to cop mode, and he scrambled out into the yard. By that time, J.D. had escaped Double H's headlock and was riding the portly biker like a pregnant sow.

"Let him go!" Winky yelled. "Double H is our friend, J.D.!"

"Break it up, you two," Tom barked, and hoisted J.D. off Double H's back. The diminutive attorney kicked his legs in the air like he was riding an invisible bicycle.

Tom set J.D. and his Gucci loafers on the lawn, then grabbed Double H by the wrist and tugged until he was able to right his sizeable girth and the portly PI stumbled to his feet.

"What in the world is going on here?" Tom demanded, looking right at me.

I diverted my eyes to the sky in search of another miracle. Or maybe I'd get lucky and a meteor would put me out of my misery....

"Val?" Tom said sternly. "How do you know this guy?"

"He's uh...a friend of Laverne's," I said. Which, technically, was true.

As if on cue, Laverne appeared. "What's going on?" She spotted the two ruffians still panting in the yard. "You two at it again? Geeze! J.D., I told you Harvey and I are *just friends.*"

What in the world? Is there some kind of love triangle going on between Laverne, J.D. and Double H? Woo hoo! Thanks to Laverne, I don't have to explain to Tom that we hired Double H as a hitman! Yes! This really is a miracle!

"Men can be so silly," I said, nearly gasping with relief.

I scrambled for something to say that would reiterate the love triangle-theme and divert the attention off me. I turned to Laverne.

"You always look great, Laverne. It's no wonder you've got men fighting each other for you."

"Why thank you, honey," Laverne said, and demurely tugged at her skin-tight mini skirt.

"So that's what this is about," Tom said to the two brawlers. "All right, men. Shake hands and let's take this inside."

J.D. and Double H did as they were told, and we all adjourned to Winky's living room, where the 1970s was putting up its own desperate fight for survival.

"WERE THEY REALLY FIGHTING over Laverne?" Tom asked me.

We were sitting on Winky's red-and-orange plaid couch. Everyone had gone to get more beer, so we had a moment alone – unless I counted E.T. the Extraterrestrial. He was sitting in a pie plate, staring at me from under a lampshade. I pondered for a second how on earth to change the red lightbulb in the center of his chest, when his little blinking heart-light finally blew out.

"I guess so, Tom. But I don't know for sure. I mean, I barely know Double H."

"Speak of the devil," Tom said.

"Sorry about the disturbance earlier," Double H said. He plopped onto the couch beside me, creating a crater that swept me up in its vortex. I grabbed an armrest and righted myself.

Tom and Double H nodded silent acknowledgements, then Double H turned to me.

"Don't mean to barge in. Val, I just wanted to give you something." He reached into his pocket and pulled out a clear baggie. Inside it were about a dozen frizzy, reddish- brown hairs.

"I forgot to give you the Finkerman samples," he said.

Tom's hand clamped down on my thigh, just above my knee. I didn't dare look at him. Instead, I kept my focus on Double H and tucked the baggie into my purse.

"Uh...thank you," I said matter-of-factly. "Mr. Hooters, Tom and I were just wondering. What's your problem with J.D.? Are you interested in Laverne?"

"Huh?" Double H asked, his brows furrowing. "Oh. You mean when she said.... Listen, I didn't want to hurt her feelings or nothin'. Laverne's a great gal and all. But she's way too skinny for me."

"So then, what's your beef with J.D.?" Tom asked.

"Don't say nothing, 'cause Winky doesn't know it yet. But it turns out that J.D.'s the jerk that's been giving Winky a hard time. With the loitering charges, I mean."

Tom shot me a suspicious look. So far, I'd been able to explain away everything that had gone on without incriminating myself. I had a sinking feeling my luck wasn't going to hold.

"And Val," Double H continued, "I been meaning to let you know. I seen J.D. snooping around your house earlier this week. I'm telling you, that little guy's up to no good."

The lazy gerbil in my mind climbed onto its wobbly wheel. "What do you mean, J.D. was sneaking –"

"Shh!" Double H hissed. "Winky's coming. I owe it to him to tell him first."

"But you already told *us*," Tom said dryly.

"Oops," Double H said. "I trust you'll keep it on the down-low. Last thing we need is some *cop* finding out."

Double H hoisted his massive gut off the couch and headed toward Winky, who was busy chatting up Jorge and his girlfriend Sherryl.

"Well?" Tom asked.

I looked at him sheepishly.

"Nice lamp," I said.

Tom wasn't amused.

Chapter Forty-Four

"Let me get this straight," Tom said. He'd led me into Winky's backyard for a private discussion. I was cornered by the hot tub and about to get into some seriously hot water.

"You traded all my stuff away for *figurines?*" Tom said, his sea-green eyes storming.

"No," I offered weakly. "We also had Chinese...."

"Val! How could you?"

"Well, *you* sold Goober's dreamcatcher to Finkerman!"

Tom's face softened a tad. He blew out a breath and said, "Okay. Go on. Tell me the rest. *All* of it."

I swatted at a mosquito buzzing around my face and wished I had a gin and tonic instead of a Pabst Blue Ribbon.

"Well, when I found out Finkerman had Goober's dreamcatcher, I decided to pay him a visit. In disguise. As...well, you saw it. As Destiny."

Tom looked hurt. "So our little role-playing date wasn't real?"

I looked up at Tom with puppy-dog eyes. "It seemed real enough to me."

Tom looked away. "Then what happened?"

"I went to Finkerman's office, but the dreamcatcher wasn't there. Then Winky called saying this lady named Layla Lark was offering a twenty-grand reward for the Dr. Dingbat's figurine."

"But why in the world were you scrounging around in a dumpster?"

I tried to take Tom's hand, but he shooed it away.

"When I met with Layla, she told me the blasted figurine wasn't worth ten bucks without the original battery. You see, Tom, Winky had replaced the old battery the day before. When I showed it to him at the donut shop."

"Why'd he replace the battery?"

"Because it didn't work."

"Work?"

"The figurine wouldn't...you know...grunt."

Tom bit his lip.

"Well, I figured twenty grand was a lot of money to just toss out the window. So I got in the dumpster to try and find the old battery. But I was too late."

Tom looked horrified. "Okay," he said. "Fair enough. I get that part. But how did that private eye, Double H get tangled up in this? And J.D.? And what's with the baggie full of hair?"

I cringed. "Well, that's where it gets a little complicated. Finkerman slapped me with a lawsuit for intent to do bodily harm...you know, for Laverne's digestive-suicide cookies. He was also extorting Laverne for an overdue library book. So we hired Double H as a...hit man."

Tom choked on his beer. "A *hit man?*"

"Not like a *real* hit man!" I said. "More like a 'hair-removal man.' Just to get Finkerman to drop the charges, see?"

Tom stared at me for a moment. I pulled out the baggie of hair. When Tom put two and two together, the sum made his eyes bulge.

"Of all your lame-brained ideas, Val! This one takes the cake!"

"More like the follicle," I said, trying to make a joke.

Tom didn't laugh.

"Okay, okay," I said. "But everything worked out in the end, Tom. It's over with Finkerman. In fact, this whole mess is settled. Except for the break-in. And Goober's dreamcatcher, of course. It's gone for good."

"Look Val," Tom began, then stopped. "Wait a minute. The break in?"

I tried to shrug, but it came off more like a nervous tick. "Someone broke into the house on Wednesday. They stole a figurine and some Halloween candy. No biggie."

Tom's face turned to sludge. "Geeze, Val! I'm so sorry. I had no idea that this –"

"There they are!" Milly's voice rang out. "It's the soon-to-be puppy parents!"

"Hey, you two," her husband Vance said, and shook Tom's hand. "What's new with you and Val?"

Tom looked me in the eye and said, "Nothing, Vance. Absolutely nothing."

I grimaced out a smile and asked, "Can I get anybody a beer?"

"LET ME HELP YOU WITH that," I said to J.D. He was standing on the bottom shelf of Winky's fridge, trying to reach a case of beer.

"Thanks, Val," he said, and stepped back down to the floor.

"What's your pleasure?" I asked.

"Heineken, if he's got it."

"Looks like it's PBR or PBR."

"I'll take a Pabst, then," he said, and ran a hand through his silver hair.

I handed J.D. the beer and couldn't help but notice that the usually immaculately dressed attorney looked a bit disheveled this evening. Grass stains marred the right shoulder of his white dress shirt like green skid marks, and the knees of his expensive-looking pants were as dirty as a six-year-old's after recess.

"Thanks. I owe you one," he said, and cracked open the beer.

"You sure do," I said. "Help me find Goober and I won't say a word to Laverne that I know it was you."

J.D.'s face froze. "How did you figure it out?"

"Double H told me."

"Oh. I thought maybe you'd spotted the chocolate stain on my pocket."

I cocked my head at J.D. "Huh?"

"Please, I'm begging you, Val. Don't say another word about it. Laverne will throw me out of her life for good if she finds out."

Unsure as to just what J.D. was confessing to, I asked a generic question to fish for more information.

"So, why'd you do it, J.D.?"

"I just *had* to have Su Mee back. Listen, Val, I'm sorry for breaking in your place. I'll do anything I can to help you find Goober...you know, to make up for it."

"Su Mee?" I squealed. "I was talking about the loitering complaint you filed against Winky!"

J.D. turned the color of olive loaf. "Oh."

"J.D.! Don't tell me *you're* the one who broke in and rifled through my closet. J.D., you *stole* from me!"

"I know, I know!" J.D. confessed. "But only Su Mee, Val. And only for sentimental reasons. You see, Laverne sold it at the yard sale without my permission."

"Oh," I said.

"I kind of lost it," he confessed. "I'll pay you for it."

"It's okay, J.D.," I said, my outrage waning a bit. "You can have Su Mee. Just tell me something. How did you know I had her?"

"Laverne told me she'd sold Su Mee to some guy, along with a bunch of other things of mine. It was like a punch in the gut, Val. I was really upset with her."

"I can understand that."

"Anyway, later Laverne mentioned seeing you with Su Mee...in a box with some other figurines. Well, knowing your penchant for smashing them, I knew Su Mee wouldn't last a week at your place."

I bit my lip. I couldn't argue with that.

"I came over and knocked on your door, but you weren't home," J.D. said. "I got so worried about losing Su Mee that I decided to sneak in the back window. It was unlocked, you know. Anyway, I searched every box I could find in your place. I got lucky and found her. And, well, I took her. I'm sorry."

"But Su Mee. She's so...*tacky,* J.D. And you're so...well...*not.*"

J.D. blew out a breath. "I know. But my dearly departed mother gave Su Mee to me when I graduated law school. It's all I've got left of her."

"Oh." I put my hand on J.D.'s shoulder. "I get it. Well, you're welcome to her, okay?"

"Thanks, Val."

"But I don't get why you didn't just ask me for her."

J.D. looked down at the floor.

"I was ashamed. And then, after the break in...well, I took your chocolate ghosts. For that, I have no excuse, Val. But you know how bad Laverne's cooking is. I saw the candy and I guess I just snapped. Out of hunger. And stress."

"I totally get it."

J.D. looked up at me.

"Did I mention Laverne sold my custom-made Armani suits in the yard sale? Someone got fifteen grand worth of suits for fifteen bucks."

"Ouch."

"I guess I deserved it. Do you forgive me, Val?"

I sighed and let out a tired laugh.

"Yeah. I guess we all do crazy things for love. And from the looks of you, J.D., you've suffered enough. I won't say a word to Laverne about the break in *or* the loitering thing. So long as you don't bother Winky anymore."

"Thank you," J.D. said, and extended his hand. I let it go and hugged him instead.

"Like I said, I promise I'll do my best to help you find Goober."

"Thanks, J.D. Listen, I better get going." I opened the fridge and grabbed a carton off the top shelf. "I'm way overdue on my beer delivery route."

"Okay," he said. "I better go have a talk with Double H before he gets to Winky. I'll let him know I won't be filing any more complaints."

Chapter Forty-Five

"I'll take one of those," Vance said as I came into the living room toting a six-pack of PBRs.

I passed the beers around, then plopped down on the couch in between Tom and Milly. Winnie and Winky were in front of us, lounging like a pair of lazy bookends in their matching arm chairs.

"I think what you two need is a new puppy," Milly said to Winnie, and winked at her.

"Well, I don't know," Winnie said. "We've got so much going on right now, what with the new house and the wedding to plan."

"And a hearse to drive," Tom quipped.

Winky laughed. "That's right! It's hard to be on the road yard salin' with a puppy at home."

"Take it with you!" Milly said. "The puppies love to ride in the car."

"What about in a hearse?" Winky asked.

"Sure," Milly said. "And it just so happens, I've got two puppies left. A boy and a girl."

Winkie turned to Winnie. "What 'a you think, Princess? You ready for a new addition to the family?"

Winnie smiled. "Why not. The more the merrier, right?"

"We'll take 'em both," Winky said.

"Perfect!" Milly said. "What will you call them?"

"Well, if'n it's all right with my darlin' here, I think we should name 'em after Val."

"Me?" I said.

"Yep," Winky said. "Miss fancy mystery writer, what'd'ya thank about Nancy Drew and Hardy Boy?"

I shook my head and laughed. "I think it's bloody genius, Winky."

Tom took my hand and smiled. "While you're all here, I have an announcement to make, too," he said.

Everyone looked his way. Tom gripped my hand firmly and said, "I just wanted to make it official. Val has lost our little wager. My Barcalounger stays."

My head snapped around. "What are you talking about, Tom?"

"It's simple, Val. You smashed a figurine. You lost."

"But...I thought we agreed, Tom. Dropping that pizza guy on the floor didn't count."

"No. But *this* does."

Tom reached in his shirt pocket and handed me something. My eyebrows raised an inch.

It was the little slip of paper from inside the Dr. Dingbat figurine. I'd thrown it away in Jake's garbage bin – along with the shattered remains of Doo-Doo Daddy.

"Where'd you get this?" I asked, and looked up at Tom. His face was unreadable.

"I have my sources," he said.

Right. And they're named Jake Johnson.

"I *bet* you do," I muttered. "But so what? NIM 1 is just the name of some Chinese factory inspector, Tom. I'm sure the poor guy's had to inspect millions of figurines. This doesn't prove a thing."

Tom shook his head. "Geeze, Val. Turn the paper the other way around."

When I turned the paper upside down, it read, "I WIN."

My line of vision zeroed in on Tom. The rest of the world fell away.

"Wait a minute..." I said. But I couldn't hear myself over the din.

Everyone was laughing.

At me.

"That's right, Val," Tom said, a sly grin plastered on his lips. "You've been set up."

"Had," Milly said.

I looked, one by one, at my circle of friends.

"Tricked," Vance said.

"Conned," Jorge said.

"Duped," Sherryl said.

"Outsmarted," Laverne said.

"Deceived," J.D. said.

"Hoodwinked," Winnie said.

"Bamboozled," Winky said, and waggled his ginger eyebrows.

The circle completed, my eyes returned to Tom.

"But...how?" I stammered.

"You forget. I'm a detective."

"With a good back-up team," Jorge added.

I shook my head slowly. "The Dr. Dingbat figurine...wasn't *real?*"

"Nope," Tom said.

"Ha ha! We got you good!" Winky said.

My gut relaxed, as if everything inside me had suddenly given up all hope. I felt as if I were hovering somewhere outside my own body.

How could I have been so utterly fooled?

"The figurine of a guy on a toilet was my idea," Tom said.

His voice sounded as if it were underwater. I watched as Tom high-fived Jorge and said, "Didn't I tell you she wouldn't be able to resist?"

"Tom told me what he wanted," Laverne's voice rang out loud and clear, bursting the water-bubble effect. "I had a buddy from my old ceramics class make it" Laverne beamed at me. "Wasn't that a great idea, honey?"

"You were in on it too?" I asked, still stunned with disbelief.

I shook my head again and muttered, "I should have known something was up when you made that comment about it taking a dingbat to know a dingbat."

The old lady smiled at me brightly. "It sure does, sugar!"

"I'm the one wanted it to grunt," Winky said. "So I got Jorge to wire it up for sound."

Jorge laughed. "I guess you've probably figured out by now that Winky provided the sound effects."

As the shock began to wear off, I realized, in hindsight, that clues had been everywhere.

I should have known something was up when Winky knew what the term 'defecation' meant.

"Wait a minute," I said. "What about the ad in Craigslist?"

"Totally made up." Milly said, raising a finger. "By me, I might add."

"But Layla Lark," I protested. "She was real."

"My great aunt," Sherryl said.

"The figurine...it was on Nancy's yard-sale table. How'd you get *her* to play along?"

Tom shrugged. "Nancy was happy to help...in exchange for the name of the person who left those black tire tracks in her driveway."

"Traitor!" I hissed at Tom. "You let me dive in a dumpster for nothing! I could've gotten hepatitis!"

Tom cringed. "I know. I'm sorry. I had no idea *that* was going to happen. It was totally off script. The whole 'wrong battery' thing was improvised by Layla."

"She can be a bit sadistic," Sherryl said and shrugged apologetically. "What can I say? She's a Scorpio."

I turned my wrath toward Winky. "But *you* knew the battery was worthless! And you still let me scrounge around in that filthy dumpster for half an hour!"

Winky shrunk back, his face one big grimace surrounded by freckles.

"Sorry, Val pal. But I couldn't do nothin' about it."

"Why not?"

"You see, when I called Layla to let her know you was on your way, I just happened to mention the battery was dead and I'd changed it out. Well, I guess she run wild with it. Right after your meetin' with her, Layla called me. She told me she'd upped the prank by telling you the figure was worthless without the original battery.

"Well, by that point, Val, you was already pullin' up in the parkin' lot. I couldn't do nothin' but play along else'n I'd a ruined the whole thang."

Winky smiled apologetically. "On the bright side, at least I got you outta the dumpster a'fore they dumped you into the truck."

"Yeah. Thanks," I muttered.

I shook my head and stared at the group snickering around me.

"Am I really that easy a mark?" I asked.

Tom snorted. "So easy, Val, it's scary."

Chapter Forty-Six

I would have liked to say that I'd been a good sport about the whole prank thing. But that would've been a lie. I was as bad a sport as had ever been aired on ESPN.

In fact, when everyone got done telling their side of the story, I do believe my anger could only have been measured on a Richter scale.

I'd been fooled by Tom. That was bad enough. But I'd also been duped by the gang of people I'd thought were my loyal friends.

Outsmarted by Laverne and Winky? Geeze!

That had been too much for my Southern pride to bear. Even worse, the trick I'd fallen for had doomed me to have to look at Tom's ugly chair for the rest of my life. Now there would be a daily reminder that I'd been played for a chump – *by a figurine taking a dump.*

"You okay, Val?" Milly asked.

"Sure," I lied, and laughed bitterly as an iron fist clamped around my heart.

Tom and the rest of you just made a fool out of me. I'm perfectly fine, Milly. Hunky dory. Peachy keen.

Then a thought occurred to me that made me feel even worse – something I hadn't thought was possible.

Maybe they hadn't *made me into a fool. Maybe they'd only given me enough rope to do it myself....*

219

As I stood in the circle along with the people I'd thought were my friends, something broke inside me. Or sealed up. I couldn't decide. Was I too sensitive? Or were they too *in*sensitive?

All I knew for sure was that the camaraderie I'd felt earlier in the evening had evaporated. A thick void had taken its place – a barrier between "me" and "them" as tangible to me as a concrete wall.

"You gotta admit, we got you good," Jorge said, breaking me out of my inner machinations.

"Yes. Good one," I said. "Excuse me for a moment."

I stepped out of the room. Everyone continued to talk and laugh as I calmly walked down the hall and into the kitchen.

By the time I grabbed my purse off the countertop, my pulse was beating in my throat. I sprinted for the front door....

I WAS BACKING MAGGIE out of Winky's yard when Tom came running out the door.

"Wait! Val! Where are you going?" he called out.

"Home!" I hissed.

"Why?"

"Why don't you '*figure*' it out?" I yelled, and shifted Maggie into drive.

Tom's face sagged with distress. "Val! I'm sorry! I told you, I didn't mean for it –"

"Save it!" I bellowed.

"But...how will I get home?"

"They're *your* friends, Tom. I'm sure *some*body'll give you a lift."

I stomped on the gas.

Maggie's twin glass-packs roared.

The tires squealed. Burnt rubber and dust boiled up and clouded the road, until both Tom and Winky's place were completely out of sight.

NEVER AROUND WHEN I need him!

Quick streaks of shiny metal.

Thinks I'm nothing but a bumbling fool!

A sound like distant drumbeats.

Got rid of Goober's dreamcatcher!

Whooshing in my eardrums.

I bet an old girlfriend gave it to him!

My Hammer of Justice came down on Tom's old Barcalounger like a knife blade in a shower at the Bates Motel.

I know he's keeping you just to piss me off! Well, we'll see about that!

I hammered at the hapless chair again and again and again, until I was so spent I collapsed on my knees in front of it. Despite my brutal attack, the hideous Barcalounger didn't look any worse for wear.

How was that even possible?

Tires ground on the driveway in front of the house. A car door slammed shut. I tried to stand up, but couldn't.

If I'm going to be made a fool of, I might as well let an expert do it. Forget you, Tom Foreman! In the morning, I'm packing my bags and heading to my mother's in Greenville!

Dizzy and hassling like a hound, I scrambled down the hallway on my hands and knees. I heard the front door creak open just as the office door clicked behind me. I locked the door, then leaned up against it, panting with fury and exhaustion.

A moment later, I heard Tom's voice.

"Are you all right, Val?"

I didn't answer.

Tom didn't ask again.

I dragged myself to the daybed, crawled onto it and pulled the covers up to my neck.

A voice whispered in my ear.

What are you winning, holding onto your anger?

I flung the hammer against the wall.

I don't know, Glad. But I'm afraid if I let it go, I'll disappear into nothingness....

I WOKE TO THE SMELL of cappuccino and someone tapping lightly on my office door.

"You awake in there?"

"Go away, Tom."

"I have a cappuccino for you. And something I think will make you feel a whole lot better."

I didn't answer.

"Please, Val. Give me *one* minute. That's all I ask."

I crawled out of the daybed and cracked open the door.

What Tom had in his hand made me break down and ball my eyes out.

And it wasn't a cappuccino.

Chapter Forty-Seven

"Where did you find it?" I asked, and wiped the brimming tears from my eyes.

"For the record, I never lost it," Tom said, and handed me Goober's redneck dreamcatcher.

"You didn't?" I sniffed.

"No. I hid it in the garage. Somehow, Winky found it and sold it at the yard sale when you left him in charge. I looked out the window and saw Finkerman carrying it away. I want you to know, it cost me my old boom box and a potato peeler to get it back."

"But Tom, you *lied* to me. You told me you sold it to a guy with pink glasses."

"To Finkerman."

"But Finkerman wasn't wearing those stupid glasses the second day of sale – when Winky was there."

Tom smiled at me with a mixture of guilt and pride.

"You're right. Nice work, Valiant Stranger. And yes, technically, I lied. But Finkerman *did* have the dreamcatcher...for a few minutes."

"But Tom, I was *devastated* at losing it."

"I know. I mean, I know *now*. I had no idea you would take it so hard. And after it was done, I couldn't go back. Not until, you know, the goose chase was finished."

"And I guess my goose is well and truly cooked now. Thanks."

Tom took my hand. "Val, you have to believe me. I had no idea this stupid prank would turn into such a fiasco. Do you? Believe me, I mean? I'd never do anything to intentionally hurt you."

I looked into Tom's sea-green eyes. They shone with sincerity.

"I do," I said. "But I hope you understand this means you owe me, Tom Foreman. And I mean *big time*."

A tear trailed down Tom's dimpled cheek. "Yes ma'am. What can I do to make it up to you?"

"You can start by handing me that cappuccino."

Tom laughed and handed me the cup.

I took a sip. "Not bad," I said. "Now, you can tell me why in the world you want to torture the living daylights out of me by keeping that hideous chair. Be honest with me. Did some other woman give it to you?"

"Yes," Tom said.

I shot him a hurt look. Tom shook his head and laughed.

"She was my *grandmother*, Val. But that's not the reason I want to keep the chair."

"Then what in the world *is?*"

"I was sitting in that chair the first time I asked you out...and you said 'yes.'"

Tears flooded my eyes to the brim.

"But Val, if you hate it that much, I'll get rid of it. And you can keep on smashing your figurines, if you need to. All I ask is one thing in return."

"What?"

"Snuggle with me one more time in it, before I take the old beast to the curb."

"Okay."

Tom took the cappuccino from my hand and tugged me into the living room. He set the cup on the kitchen counter, scooped me up into his arms like Prince Charming, and carried me to the chair.

Then he leaned back and fell, butt-first, into the old Barcalounger. It collapsed under our weight like a soggy cardboard box.

Tom and I tumbled downward, along with the chair's plaid-upholstered remains, until we were sprawled out on the floor.

But when the dust had settled, we were still in each other's arms.

Chapter Forty-Eight

"Here you go!" Milly said, and handed Tom a wriggling clump of white and grey fluff. "Sir Albert Snoggles, III is all yours!"

I smiled at Tom as I patted the tiny dog's head. Seeing how small the puppy was made me realize how foolish I'd been to make such a big deal out of what to call it.

In the end, I'd let Tom keep the name he'd wanted all along. It was only fair. After all, Tom really *had* won our wager.

Naming the dog Sir Albert Snoggles, III was a consolation prize Tom could live with. He had to. I'd destroyed his original ante. Somewhere in northern Pinellas County, his poor old plaid Barcalounger was making an ugly landfill even more unsightly.

Oh, well.

Tom passed me the pup. One look at precious little Albert's face convinced me everything was going to be all right. It was love at first sight.

"Uh oh!" Tom said. "Watch out!"

I heard a snarl at my ankles. I looked down to see my old nemesis, Albert's mother, Charmine. She was getting ready to nip my fledgling love for her son in the bud – or, more accurately, the ankle.

My ankle.

Milly grabbed Charmine up in her arms before she had time to chew my toes off.

"Sorry, Val," Milly said. "I guess you're right. She really *doesn't* like you."

I shrugged. "I guess you can't please everyone."

"That's right," Vance said. "If you want to be happy, you've got to please yourself."

"Or your girlfriend," I heard Tom whisper.

"Ha ha," I said, and cuddled my new companion. "Like I said before, Tom. I liked you better when you couldn't tell a joke."

Weary from an angry, fitful night spent on the daybed, I yawned. Sir Albert Snoggles, III took the opportunity to insert his little pink puppy tongue right into my mouth.

Yuck!

"Snoggles must be French," I said, trying not to gag.

"French!" Milly squealed. "The French toast!"

Milly stuffed Charmine into Vance's arms and took off for the kitchen.

"It's too early to tell," Vance said. "But we might have to go out for brunch."

"That's okay," I said to my new fur baby. "Isn't it, little Snoggly-Woggly?"

Now I had *two* guys to love.

WHEN WE PULLED UP IN the driveway with our new housemate, Sir Albert Snoggles, III, we were shocked to see J.D. throw a suitcase in the trunk of his white Mercedes and speed off.

"What's going on?" I called out.

Laverne picked her way across the lawn.

"Is that your new puppy?" she asked.

"No," Tom joked. "He's his stunt double."

"Oh," Laverne said. "Well, I bet he looks just like him."

"Right."

"Can I hold him?" she asked.

"Sure," I said, and put the pup in her arms.

"Aren't you the sweetest thing!" she cooed.

"What's up with J.D.?" I asked.

"I think we're through," Laverne said.

She shrugged and looked up from the pup toward Tom and me.

"You know, you two are lucky," she said. "Some people never do ripen up with age. They stay sour their whole lives."

I squeezed Tom's hand.

"I'm sorry, Laverne," I offered.

"Don't be. I'll be fine. Happiness is an inside job, you know."

She handed the pup over to Tom.

"Well, I better get back inside. I got a Skinny Dip dinner waiting for me. See you around!"

Laverne turned to go, then waved at someone behind us. I turned to see Jake busy pounding another sign in his yard.

"Tom, go on in with Snoggles. I want to ask Jake something."

As Tom toted the pup inside, I marched over to Jake.

"What are you doing, fraternizing with the enemy?" I demanded.

"What are you talking about?"

"I saw you with Nancy. And I heard you talking with her about Ralph."

Jake eyed me dubiously, like a jaded primate.

"So what if I talked to her. Ralph's a real handful. Nancy needed help from somebody who understood the criminal mind."

"Because Ralph's a thief?"

Jake looked at me dubiously. "How'd you know that?"

"I...uh...might have overheard some of your conversation."

"Inside Nancy's house? Geeze, Val. You're as big a busybody as *she* is."

"I am not! And I think it's illegal, what she's doing. You can't hold a man against his will like that. You of all people should know *that*, Jake!"

"Geeze, Val. If you're gonna go snooping around, you should at least get your facts straight."

"What do you mean?"

"Ralph's not a man. He's a parrot."

I STOMPED BACK TO MY house, feeling like a complete bird brain. I kicked off my sandals and stepped right into a warm puddle.

"Tom!" I yelled.

He came down the hallway toting the puppy and a pile of old newspapers.

"Sorry. I was going to put papers down, but little Snoggles here beat me to it."

"Well aren't you a little darling," I said.

Tom handed me the pup. "Watch him while I lay the newspapers around."

I carried the wriggling pup down the hallway toward the bedroom.

"So, you like to be naughty?" I asked Snoggles.

He yipped in reply.

"Okay then. Give this a go."

I reached into my secret shoebox stash and tossed a rag on the floor. Little Snoggles went wild.

"Oh, no!" I cried out.

Tom came running in. "What's wrong? Is the puppy okay?"

"Oh, Tom," I wailed. "Look what little Snoggles did to your uniform!"

As if on cue, little Albert snarled, then ripped at the already torn sleeve of Tom's ruined cop shirt.

Tom shook his head and laughed. "He's so cute, you just have to forgive him.

"I totally agree."

I picked up the ball of fluff and held him to my chest.

Yes, Sir Albert Snoggles, III, I think this is the beginning of a beautiful relationship....

FROM THE WAY TOM WAS acting, you would think he and I'd just adopted a *real* kid.

Even from my vantage point – peeking out through a slit in the living room blinds – I could see Tom beaming at Snoggles like a proud papa. Our neighbor Jake appeared equally enamored with our new canine companion.

I smiled and let go of the blinds. It had been a hectic day, but Snoggles seemed to be settling in quickly to his new surroundings. So, while Tom and the new pup weren't underfoot, I used the respite to hang up Goober's redneck dreamcatcher.

Instead of returning it to the window in the bedroom, I decided it would look better in my home office. I reached up to hook the dreamcatcher's hanger onto the curtain rod, but all I got was a beer can in the eyeball. I was too short to reach the rod by a good five inches.

I needed something to stand on.

Too lazy to drag a stool from the kitchen, I wheeled my office chair up to the side of the daybed, where I'd laid the dreamcatcher. I braced the chair against the bed, then carefully climbed into it until I was squatting with my feet in the seat and my hands on the back of the chair.

I grabbed the dreamcatcher. Then slowly, as if I were learning to ride a surfboard, I cautiously wobbled my way from squatting to standing.

So far, so good.

I held the dreamcatcher up and reached for the curtain rod....

The chair shot out from under me like a bull out of a rodeo gate. I yelped, flung the dreamcatcher across the room, and took a flying leap toward the daybed. I landed on it in a face-first belly flop.

The dreamcatcher wasn't quite as lucky.

I looked over to see it was lying on the floor in a corner, like the aftermath of a party I was glad I hadn't been invited to.

Both beer cans that'd been dangling on fishing line from the bottom of the dreamcatcher were covered in collision dents. The tin of Skoal chewing tobacco wasn't smashed, but the impact had caused it to burst open. Its lid was still rolling around in circles on the floor, making a tinny, down-the-drain kind of sound.

I climbed off the daybed and picked up the lid just as it made its final death spiral. I walked to the corner and picked up the derelict remains of the rest of the dreamcatcher.

I wiped the dust bunnies off the pink panties and was about to put the lid back on the Skoal tin when I realized there was something inside it. A slip of paper had been fastened inside with thin strips of duct tape. Written on the paper was a single word.

PObbLE

Goober had left me a clue after all!

Carefully, I peeled the paper from the duct tape. I put it on my desk and replaced the lid on the Skoal tin. After procuring a stool from the kitchen, I hung the redneck dreamcatcher in the window. It glimmered in the sunlight, none the worse for wear except for the dents.

Actually, I think they give it more character....

With the dreamcatcher in place once again, a little sigh of relief escaped my lips. I smiled and picked up the small strip of paper I'd found inside the tin.

PObbLE

What in the world could that mean?

"What'cha doin?" Tom asked, startling me enough to make me suck in a breath.

"Oh! Nothing," I said, and hid the paper behind my back. "Justin hanging up Goober's dreamcatcher. See?"

Tom looked up at the contraption made of pink panties and beer cans and smiled wistfully.

"How'd it get all banged up?" he asked.

"Uh...I dropped it," I said. "Does it look bad?"

"No worse than usual," Tom joked. He smiled, then his expression went as serious as mine.

"Don't worry, Val. We'll find him."

Tom wrapped his arms around me. "Let me help out this time, okay?"

"Yeah, sure thing," I said, and carefully tucked the tiny piece of paper away in my pocket.

DEAR READER,

Thanks so much for reading Figure Eight! Who doesn't like a good yard sale?

Or a good yarn tale....

Life is a lot like a yard sale. People and things show up at our tables whether we want them to or not – and they either stick around a while, or just eyeball us briefly and keep on walking.

And, like a karmic yard sale, sometimes it just feels good to get rid of the useless things cluttering up our lives. (I've heard that's how we make room for new ones.)

While I was writing Figure Eight, I lost a good friend. But then an old friend came back into my life. Was it coincidence? Fate? The hand of God?

I can't say for sure. But it makes me wonder if maybe we're all just table fodder in the big yard sale of life. If so, I want to be a Mr. Peanut piggy bank.

How about you?

If you'd like to know when my future novels come out, please subscribe to my newsletter. I won't sell your name or send too many notices to your inbox. Just click the link below to get started!

Newsletter Link: https://dl.bookfunnel.com/fuw7rbfx21

Also, thanks again for reading my book. Until next time, all my best!

Sincerely,

Margaret Lashley

P.S. The Val Fremden Mystery Series is coming to an end! The last book in the series, *Cloud Nine: When Pigs Fly,* is available on preorder now – just in time for Thanksgiving! Order it now with the link below:

https://www.amazon.com/dp/B07HDTXZZ2

P.S.S. I live for reviews! The link to leave yours is right here:

https://www.amazon.com/dp/B07GW4H956

P.S.S.S. (Can of Aquanet?) If you'd like to contact me, you can reach me by:

Website: https://www.margaretlashley.com

Email: contact@margaretlashley.com

Facebook: https://www.facebook.com/valandpalspage/

What's Next for Val?

First of All, Thanks for Reading Figure Eight!
    I hope you enjoyed Figure Eight: Yardsale Karma. If you did, please take a moment and leave a review now. I read and appreciate every single one!

https://www.amazon.com/dp/B07GW4H956#customerReviews

Ready for more Val? Set your sights on **Cloud Nine: When Pigs Fly**. Val and Tom are right on track, but Goober's still out in left field. The hunt is on to bring a happy conclusion to this ongoing mystery.... Say hello and goodbye to the gang in the dramatic conclusion to the Val Fremden Humorous Mystery Series.

Click the link below to get **Cloud Nine: When Pigs Fly** now!

https://www.amazon.com/dp/B07HDTXZZ2

Here's a sample of what you're in for!

Cloud Nine Excerpt

Chapter One

The scrap of paper in my hand was sticky to the touch. No bigger than the kind of note tucked inside a fortune cookie, it could've meant nothing at all. Yet, as I studied it, I couldn't help but think that the fate of a good friend might depend on the single, enigmatic word written upon it.

PObbLE

What in the world could that *mean?*

An exasperated breath forced its way from my lungs. I read the word again.

PObbLE

This has *to be a clue. Otherwise, I have pretty much* nothing *to go on.*

Nearly three weeks had passed since Goober'd rescued me from a mob of enraged campers during a writer's retreat that had gone horribly wrong.

No one had heard from him since.

I'd been the last one to see him alive. According to the law, that may've made me a suspect. But, like it or not, I answered to an even higher authority – the *Southern Guilt Guidebook*. According to *it*, I was definitely responsible.

Somehow. Someway....

I tapped a finger on my desk in the hope that knocking on fake wood laminate would change my luck, or loosen some forgotten detail lodged in the recesses of my addled brain.

I've got to be missing something.

Eighteen days ago, I'd waved goodbye to my tall, lanky friend in the parking lot of the Polk County Police Station in Lake Wales, Florida, about eighty miles east of St. Pete Beach. As a parting gesture, Goober'd waved back, and, in his uniquely goofy way, waggled his bushy eyebrows at me like a billiard cube infested with brown caterpillars.

Geeze. It seems like three years have gone by since then.

As in days past, I wracked my brain again, trying to recall anything suspicious about our last moments together. But try as I might, as far as I could tell, Goober'd given no indication anything weird had been going on. But then again, he'd always been such an odd duck. There was no way for me to be absolutely sure....

The last thing Goober'd said to me before he'd taken off had actually been a question. He'd asked me if I'd known my way home. He'd offered to let me follow him. In hindsight, I wished I'd taken him up on the offer.

But I didn't. Mainly because my access out of the parking lot had been blocked by an old hillbilly woman on a "shopper chopper."

Those were the words Charlene had used to describe the strange, customized bike she'd ridden around on. It was a tricycle, actually. Soldered onto the frame where the front wheel used to be was a full-sized grocery-shopping cart. During my stay at that RV park in Lake Wales, I'd seen Charlene use the handy front basket for toting everything from groceries to grannies.

I could still recall the earnestness on Charlene's face when she'd pulled that shopper chopper up behind my car and blocked me from backing up. The toilet-tube curlers pinned in her hair had jiggled around her jawline as she'd proffered her heartfelt apology for chasing me around the RV park with a pitchfork.

In her defense, she *had* thought I'd killed her sister's 94-year-old boyfriend, Woggles with a Tupperware container full of Laverne's snickerdoodles. It was a fair assumption, given Laverne's history with baked goods.

At any rate, Charlene's apology had delayed my leaving, and had put me about ten minutes behind Goober. In theory, I should've caught up with him before he reached the on-ramp for I-4. But I never saw him again. He'd simply vanished somewhere along State Road 60.

The thing was, he should've been easy to spot.

Goober'd been behind the wheel of a 1966 Minnie Winnie. The old RV used to belong to Glad, my biological mom. It was a hard target to miss. Still, compared to today's huge RVs, the thing wasn't much bigger than a tin can. I guess that made the fact that Goober'd left his strange clue inside another tin can kind of fitting.

I looked at it again.

PObbLE

I set the slip of paper on my desk and leaned back in my chair. My eyes shifted up toward the dreamcatcher hanging in the window of my home office. It'd been a parting gift from Goober.

Looking at the hideous thing *now*, I wondered if maybe it'd been more of a parting *shot*.

The crude, makeshift contraption was nothing more than a cheap, wire clothes hanger that'd been hand-bent into a warped circle. A pair of hot-pink thong panties stretched across the width of the circle like a frilly Mercedes logo. If *that* weren't low-rent enough, the folk artist/deviant who'd concocted it had used fishing line to tie three aluminum cans to the bottom half. Two Pabst Blue Ribbon cans and a Skoal tobacco tin dangled from the dreamcatcher like garbage snagged in a spider's web.

Definitely not the classiest gift I've ever gotten.

If the dreamcatcher had come from anyone else, I'd have thrown it in the trash. But it was from Goober. And now, it was all I had left of him.

Five days ago, when I'd first attempted to hang it in my office window, it had fallen out of my hands and crashed onto the terrazzo floor. The impact had dented the beer cans, and caused the Skoal tin to burst open. That's how I'd found the puzzling message within. It'd been duct-taped to the inside of the tobacco lid.

I took one last look at the sticky scrap of paper.

PObbLE

I sighed and placed it back inside my desk drawer.

Goober had called the hideous window decoration a "redneck dreamcatcher."

Now, all I had to do was catch a redneck with it.

ORDER YOUR COPY OF *Cloud Nine* now and discover the dramatic conclusion to the Val Fremden Mystery Series.

P.S. In the back of the book is a way to continue getting free short stories about Val and the gang! Get your copy of Cloud Nine by clicking the link below:

https://www.amazon.com/dp/B07HDTXZZ2

Don't miss out! Follow me on Amazon and BookBub and you'll be notified of the first release in my new series. (I'd tell you more, but it's a secret!)

Follow me on Amazon:

https://www.amazon.com/-/e/B06XKJ3YD8

Follow me on BookBub:

https://www.bookbub.com/search/authors?search=Margaret%20Lashley

Bye for now!

About the Author

Like the characters in my novels, I haven't lead a life of wealth or luxury. In fact, as it stands now, I'm set to inherit a half-eaten jar of Cheez Whiz...if my siblings don't beat me to it.

During my illustrious career, I've been a roller-skating waitress, an actuarial assistant, an advertising copywriter, a real estate agent, a house flipper, an organic farmer, and a traveling vagabond/truth seeker. But no matter where I've gone or what I've done, I've always felt like a weirdo.

I've learned a heck of a lot in my life. But getting to know myself has been my greatest journey. Today, I know I'm smart. I'm direct. I'm jaded. I'm hopeful. I'm funny. I'm fierce. I'm a pushover. And I have a laugh that makes strangers come up and want to join in the fun. In other words, I'm a jumble of opposing talents and flaws and emotions. And it's all good.

In some ways, I'm a lot like Val Fremden. My books featuring Val are not autobiographical, but what comes out of her mouth was first formed in my mind, and sometimes the parallels are undeniable. I drink TNTs. I had a car like Shabby Maggie. And I've started my life over four times, driving away with whatever earthly possessions fit in my car. And, perhaps most importantly, I've learned that friends come from unexpected places.

Made in the USA
Columbia, SC
18 June 2020